HELLO, BEAUTIFUL

AL GUNER

Hello, Beautiful

© 2023 Al Guner

ISBN 979-8-35092-879-2

eBook ISBN 979-8-35092-880-8

CHAPTER I

Kurt's father, Whisperer Joe West, first met Kurt's mother, Ece, during his military service in Istanbul, Turkey. During a vacation weekend, Joe decided to join a Bosphorus tour ship to explore the area. The ship's last stop before returning to dock was a small village called Anadolu Hisari. Joe jumped off the ship to see the village and found a restaurant for lunch. After a delicious meal at the Fisherman's Wharf restaurant, he decided to walk into the village and spotted a small gift shop. He entered the shop to buy some gifts for his friends and spotted a beautiful woman who happened to be the owner of the shop. Her name was Ece and they became friends over time, eventually falling in love and getting married. After the end of Joe's service, they settled in Joe's hometown of Tucson, Arizona, at his small ranch.

Kurt's father was a horse whisperer, hence his name. He was good at his job. After a couple of years in Tucson, Kurt's mother became pregnant with Kurt. During Kurt's younger days with his family, he helped with the family's ranch, went to school, rode horses with his father, hiked, and played guitar. He enjoyed talking to the animals he saw on his hikes, regardless of whether they were listening. Their ranch was in the heart of the wildlife with plentiful wild desert animals Tucson, Arizona, and Kurt enjoyed talking to the dogs, bunnies, roadrunners, bobcats and javelinas. Kurt's favorites bobcats were not good listeners. Their visit was always short. After high school, Kurt was accepted to the university in Tucson. He successfully finished his undergraduate studies there and was then accepted to the university's medical school with several scholarships.

Kurt's parents were very helpful, both financially and emotionally. A year before Kurt was set to graduate medical school, they lost Ece to cancer. This was a big loss for Kurt and Joe. She was a beautiful, kind, smart and hardworking woman. After the loss of his wife, Joe fell into a deep depression. As a result, Kurt's performance in school during his final year was not as good as in the previous years, but he graduated on time anyway.

With time, Joe's depression got worse, and Kurt lost his father shortly after his mother's death.

During his last year in medical school, when Kurt began considering where he wanted to go for residency, he decided he wanted to pursue his training in Europe. He was always concerning how the cowboys were enduring broken jaws and broken face, and the long painful healing process, therefore he decided to apply maxillofacial surgery residency in Graz, Austria. Karl Franzens university maxillofacial surgery gained its reputation after second world war and became one of the best maxillofacial programs in the world. Before medical school graduation, Kurt received his acceptance letter. Finally, Kurt was beginning to receive some good news again.

Given his imminent move to Europe, Kurt quickly began looking for a farmer to manage their family farm and found a nice family from Texas.

Before leaving the ranch to the farmhand and his family, Kurt decided to spend a final few days there. He spent that time reminiscing about his childhood at the ranch.

CHAPTER II

Kurt was a lonely cowboy; he didn't have friends. But he had his horses, cows, dogs and other animals around the ranch. Kurt wasn't sure if they listened to him or understood him, but he still talked to them. He found it calming to talk to these animals. The roadrunners would slow down and look at Kurt when he started talking. The quails were always in a rush, but they would make sure to give attention to him. The bunnies were always sprinting and paid no attention to Kurt. The bobcats maintained a distance, and they were not good listeners. The mountain lions were feral, and they never got close to Kurt. The javelinas hung around with the family; they were slow, and they never paid attention to Kurt. The diamondback rattlesnakes would rattle by and have no interest in listening, and Kurt would respectfully walk away from them.

This was how they had been since Kurt's childhood. No matter how the animals might have felt, Kurt always loved them. When he was studying in his room, the bobcats would sit on the wall outside his window and stare at him. At that moment, he would take a break and tell them about his plans—about how he would travel around the world. The bobcats were not good listener animals when Kurt stare them they were running a way. They probably had no interest in Kurt's future they were not listening anyway.

Their pool was an oasis amid the desert for the wild animals. On hot days, roadrunners would come to drink water from the pool.

After supper, Kurt would go to the barn to clean and feed the horses. The horses were quiet and calm. Like his father, Kurt had a good relationship with horses, and he always loved riding around with them.

The night sky was magnificent in Arizona. You could count every star. Around midnight, the coyotes would start howling. They were noisy, and Kurt couldn't talk to them anyway. When he complained about them to his parents, they would laugh at him.

Kurt and his parents spent the weekends hiking, walking, or horseback riding in the desert. Sometimes, when they were walking together, gazelles would cross their path. They were fast animals, but they would sense where the danger was coming from. When they slowed down, Kurt would start telling them about his complaints regarding his schoolteacher or his homework assignments. His parents would respectfully step aside and wait for Kurt. They would start their walks before sunrise and return to the ranch after sunset.

Kurt's father was a good horse trainer and whisperer. Sometimes he would take Kurt to go horseback riding together and have him help train the horses.

Joe was sought after by other ranchers, and Kurt and Ece helped. When they got home from a long day of work, Kurt would begin working on his schoolwork. Given all his responsibilities, Kurt didn't have time to make any friends other than with the animals who surrounded him in the desert. If Kurt had some problems, he had animal friends to listen to him. He shared his sorrows with them as well as his happiness.

During his middle school years, Kurt started to play the guitar. In the beginning, he was interested in country music. He would play guitar at the end of the day, after completing all his tasks. His biggest fan was his mom. She would come out to the porch and listen to him quietly with a smile on her face. She always took care of Kurt and Joe very well. Kurt and Joe knew they were lucky to have her in their lives and loved her very much. She left her family and her country to move to the United States with Joe West to build a family of her own in Tucson. Kurt never heard his mother complain. She was a good cook and made both Turkish and American food. Kurt wanted to visit Istanbul to see Ece's family.

Kurt's guitar skills improved with time. Kurt did not tell his classmates in school that he played the guitar. He was pretty sure classmates would make fun of him, and they would tease him like "such a weirdo Kurt plays guitar". Some nights, when he was playing his guitar on the porch, a pack of javelinas would pass through. They were not disturbed by Kurt's music, but they were not entertained either.

While in high school, Kurt started to gain an interest in jazz after his mother and father bought him a Gibson electric guitar. Having a Gibson electric guitar was good motivation for Kurt. He started to play jazz music more and more. He wasn't good, but he was okay and getting better. He couldn't play jazz alone and started a jazz group with some of his high school classmates. They started to play together every week and made good progress. Unfortunately, none of the other students had an interest in listening to jazz music. During his undergraduate years, Kurt found a jazz club in downtown Tucson, and he started to play there Friday and Saturday nights. He was generating additional income for his education.

Kurt enjoyed playing music after school; it was a form of relaxation for him. He continued to play at the jazz club through college. The jazz club eventually closed, and Kurt could not manage to play while a medical student. So Kurt went back to playing his guitar at the ranch. He enjoyed spending his weekends as a medical student at the ranch, enjoying his mother's cooking, horseback riding with Joe West, and speaking with the horses, bobcats, quails and whoever else came to the ranch to visit Kurt. Neither Ece nor Joe ever treated Kurt like an unusual child. In fact, they were very respectful of his friendship with the animals. The entire family felt a deep love for animals, a love that developed after years of growing together.

CHAPTER III

When it came to friendships with girls, Kurt wasn't so lucky. During his high school years, he was busy with heavy ranch tasks. He did not have a chance to join other kids after school hours. Kurt did have a couple of girlfriends during his high school years, but the relationship didn't last long. His lifestyle wasn't appealing. The girls were more interested in boyfriends that they could go to lunch, dinner parties or concerts with. He couldn't afford these activities financially or emotionally. Besides all of this, his interest in jazz and his talking to animals discouraged friendships. The other students were probably thinking, "What kind of weirdo is he?" Kurt was just a different person with a different lifestyle.

During his college years, Kurt started to get together with a fellow classmate named Erin. She was a good-looking blonde California girl. Tucson was a smaller, more affordable college city compared to many of the cities in California, and this was alluring to out-of-state students like Erin. She had a beautiful, athletic body. She was funny and smart. After a good start with Erin, the relationship quickly ran into turbulence. She wasn't a fan of jazz, and she was more of a city girl. She never liked Kurt's family ranch and his lifestyle. Plus, his unconditional love of animals wasn't of interest to her. She always wanted Kurt's complete attention on her. One day

Kurt told her, "You're probably right about our relationship. I should try to change."

She said, "You should work harder."

Eventually, Kurt slowly decreased his ranch workload and spent less time with his guitar and with the animals. As a result, his relationship with Erin starts to improve a little bit. Erin began spending a little more time at Kurt's family ranch. She began learning to horseback ride from Kurt. She invited Kurt to her family's house in San Diego, California, for spring break. Her father was a former navy officer who had retired to Coronado Island. Their house was near the ocean and being close to the ocean was a motivation for her. She became a good swimmer, surfer since elementary school than she joins her middle, and high school swim team, after she joins university swim team. According to Kurt, their activities were not in alignment and their differences were too great to bridge.

Their spring vacation on Coronado Island, San Diego, started with good weather. Meeting Erin's parents was a more official ordeal than meeting Kurt's parents. Erin's parents had a lot of friends and were always hanging out at their country club. They enjoyed playing golf, cards and other such activities. Erin and Kurt would wake up early in the morning to catch the surf for Erin. Kurt would sit and watch her and the beautiful ocean view. This was the first time Kurt had left the state of Arizona. He was trying to enjoy the trip as much as he could.

After they came back to school in Tucson, their relationship started to take a setback again. Erin wasn't happy with Kurt's efforts to improve their relationship. Kurt was thinking, "I can't change more than this. I can't get in a mold just because Erin wants me like that." They started to see each other less and less. Then one day Erin asked

Kurt to lunch. Kurt was anticipating the inevitable separation and said okay. They met at a quiet restaurant on University Boulevard. After several awkward minutes, Erin started to list the issues with their relationship. Kurt never blamed her. She was right if you looked at it from her side. Kurt figured she had made up her mind to end the relationship anyway. Kurt politely accepted responsibility and took a break from her. Kurt was sad because he was a lonely person. It wasn't easy for him to start a new relationship. He saw Erin several times on campus. She was hanging around other boys. She looked happy without Kurt. Kurt was a good-looking man—a man that women desired physically —but socially, he wasn't most women's type. He didn't have a nice car; instead, he drove an old Ford truck. He didn't have extra money to take girls out on nice dates. After Erin left, Kurt went back to his comfort zone with his old truck and the ranch that smelled like manure to spend time with his family and his good friends, the animals. He was happy again with all he had.

CHAPTER IV

There were a lot of female students in medical school, but Kurt didn't want to have another Erin incident. He became a harder-working student while in medical school because he always wanted to become a doctor. During his medical school years, he couldn't go off to help his family at the ranch. During his third year of medical school, Kurt's mom was diagnosed with kidney cancer. It was discovered late. She was not the type to complain, probably because she didn't want to disrupt the daily activities at the ranch during Kurt's absence. Her kidney cancer metastasized to her lungs quickly. Joe and Kurt lost their angel and the pillar of their home. This was a big setback for Kurt. Ece knew something was wrong with her health, and she was waiting for Kurt's graduation from medical school to celebrate before she dies. After the loss of his mother, Kurt gave all his attention to medical school.

After a while, Kurt's father Joe fell into a depression. Joe loved Ece very much; he missed her companionship, as they had never left each other's side since moving to Tucson. Kurt witnessed his father's health deteriorate over time. Doctors were treating him with medication and therapy, but Joe wasn't recovering. After some time, he developed lung cancer. Joe never fought back to become healthy again. Soon after losing his mother, Kurt lost his father.

Now, hard times and loneliness were on the horizon for Kurt, and he was truly alone. He still needed to complete medical school while taking on the responsibility of the ranch, both financially and physically. Kurt transferred the ranch to the renters from Texas. He picked a family friend who was a real estate broker to represent him, collect rent and do the necessary repairs at the ranch.

CHAPTER V

As his farewell to Tucson grew closer, Kurt started to get sad and anxious. Joe's friend, a neighbor rancher, arranged a farewell party at the country bar and invited several more neighbors to the party. The party was held two days prior to Kurt's departure to Graz, Austria. All the neighbors politely wanted to know why Kurt would go to Austria for residency. For Kurt, there wasn't an easy answer. First, the furthest he had ever traveled was San Diego, California. Secondly, he wanted to go out of his comfort zone and show himself there is a different world out there. Thirdly, he wanted to get good training in maxillofacial surgery, and one of the best programs was in Graz, Austria.

They drank beer and had lively conversations throughout the night. They then invited Kurt to play some country music for them. Kurt played a few of his songs, and a few popular country songs. Kurt stayed at a Tucson airport hotel his last night because he had a long flight from Tucson to Graz, Austria. He would have to switch planes twice. While he sat in the hotel lobby, he checked the Graz map. Graz wasn't a big city. Kurt liked that very much. The place he rented in Graz was very close to the medical school hospital, and the maxillofacial surgery department. Although he had studied German in high school and university, he would need to improve it in Graz. Kurt didn't want to buy a car in Graz, and instead he rented a place within walking distance of the hospital. Graz had good public transportation.

The flight to Graz took twenty-two hours after some delays. Kurt was tired, and he took a taxicab to his one-bedroom place. He called his landlord before leaving the airport and when the cab arrived at Kurt's new address, the landlord was waiting for him there. He showed the one-bedroom apartment to Kurt. The apartment was lightly furnished, with a small kitchen that contained all the appliances, and a bathroom with a shower. This was a big difference from the spacious ranch in Tucson. After taking a hot shower, he slept twelve hours, then took another shower to wake up. Kurt's apartment was close to the small forest belonging to the university and hospital complex. Kurt could walk amongst the trees to go to the clinic. He walked in the forest for a couple of hours, but he didn't see any animals other than birds. He was hoping to see some different animals in this forest. After a long walk, he found a place to have lunch and shop. The street was a beautiful historic avenue lined with restaurants, stores and cafes. He saw a pub and entered. It was crowded and noisy. People stared at him as he entered, probably because he was dressed like a cowboy. He ordered a Kruger and a bratwurst. The beer was from a local brewery established in 1495. The lunch was delicious. He decided to go grocery shopping and found a food market parallel to the main street. He bought frozen dinners, some eggs and salad. Then he took a walk to the tram. Most buildings in Graz were historic and very well taken care of. When he returned to his one-bedroom apartment, he decided to start reading the resident's guide to maxillofacial surgery. The following day he woke up early, took a shower and had a cup of coffee before walking to the clinic.

CHAPTER VI

Kurt took a deep breath, then stepped into the maxillofacial surgery department. Some of the other residents were already there by the time Kurt had arrived. They usually accepted four residents to the program per year, and all four were male. The residency director, Professor Schrolle, arrived right on time. He appeared to be a very serious director. He introduced all four residents to each other, then he took them on a tour of the clinic while also introducing them to the other residents, the nurses and the staff. During the lunch break, they went to the cafeteria in the middle of the complex. The other three first-year residents were Austrian citizens and they spoke German. In the afternoon, they met with Professor Kohle and Professor Eskinci. Professor Kohle was a very famous maxillofacial surgeon, like Eskinci. They both were well known in Europe, and beyond. They were very polite and encouraging. Kurt was also pleased to see that nobody made fun of his American accent. After listening to the professors' encouraging speeches, they met with the second-, third- and fourth-year residents. There were only two female residents in the program, and the rest were male. That first evening they all met at a famous beer hall in the city. After the first beer they began to talk about their hobbies. They were all hikers and skiers and Kurt assumed they were probably all good athletes. Kurt realized that he should quickly learn how to ski so he could fit in with the group. Two of the residents were musi-cians like Kurt. It was Kurt's turn to introduce himself next. He told them succinctly, "I am a cowboy, a horse whisperer and trainer, and I play the guitar." They all looked at him with a smile. This was the night that started his four-year residency in Graz.

The first day of work as a resident started the next day with a bang. Eskinci was very skillful and helpful. He inspired Kurt from the very first day with his skillful hands. Later, they would become good friends. The days passed quickly, and the training program was challenging. Kurt usually ate his lunch at the cafeteria and that would keep him full enough until going to bed. A year into the rigorous training program, Eskinci included Kurt on his on-call list so they both could operate together at night on-calls. Eskinci liked Kurt's desire to do a good job during his long and strenuous surgical pro-cedures. Some operations would last six hours or more. After some time, Eskinci allowed Kurt to be primary surgeon on cases, as he had full confidence in Kurt's surgical technique.

On occasional weekends he had a chance to sleep in and rest at home. He was a light sleeper since he was a kid, but the maxillofa-cial surgeries required sharp focus. On the weekends he was off, he thought about how lonely he was. His apartment was very small, and he had no opportunity to play guitar there. The apartment complex itself was very quiet. He saw by chance couple neighbors walking around, and they were old. Probably any noise was not welcome.

CHAPTER VII

After a particularly difficult operation, Kurt went to the cafeteria to have lunch and a hot coffee while he sat and rested for a while. He thought about his ranch, his family, the horses and the other animals. While he was daydreaming, a blonde Austrian woman sat across from him. Her eyes were blue, and her face had the typical Stiermark beauty. "Steirmark was a State in Austria and Steirmark woman had beautiful woman reputation" Kurt said "hello" and introduced himself by saying, "I am Kurt."

She replied by saying, "Hi, I'm Mia."

Kurt knew she could tell he wasn't from Austria. Kurt said, "I am a second-year maxillofacial surgery resident" to which she replied," I am a first-year internal medicine resident." During their conversation, Kurt told her he was from Tucson, Arizona. Like the other Austrians, she looked at his face and smiled. Kurt thought, "This must be a typical reaction they give to people coming from the United States or other countries." She asked for the ketchup bottle. Kurt remembered the magic trick his father taught him with beer cans. Kurt used his father's disappearing and reappearing magic trick while handing the ketchup bottle to Mia and she continued to smile. While he was revealing the plastic bottle, he accidentally squeezed the bottle and some of the ketchup spilled on Mia's scrubs. Mia was a calm woman who didn't make a big deal about it. She finished her lunch and bid Kurt farewell. Kurt didn't know what to say in response.

From that day onwards, Kurt was always on the lookout for Mia, but he didn't see her for a while. One day when he was sitting at the back entrance to the cafeteria, a beautiful hand put a glass ketchup bottle in front of Kurt. Kurt turned his head and saw Mia standing in front of him with a beautiful smile on her face. They both started to laugh. Kurt pulled out a chair for her and offered for her to sit. They sat in the cafeteria for some time and talked about all kinds of things. He found out that she was a skier, ice skater and played the cello in the Graz community orchestra. Kurt told her he was a horseback rider but had had no opportunity to ride in Graz so far. He told Mia he was a guitar player as well.

They both had a good time during the lunch break. Before they returned to work Kurt asked Mia if she wanted to go out to dinner over the weekend. She agreed and they decided to go to an authentic Austrian restaurant. They spent the evening learning about each other. Kurt found out that Mia had a friend in the orchestra who played classical guitar and taught at the same time. Kurt decided to get classical guitar lessons so he could play guitar and see Mia more often at community music hall where she was practicing cello. A couple of days later Mia came to visit Kurt at the maxillofacial surgery department. Shwester Betty and Elisabeth, the chief nurses, were there too. Mia stayed to chat for some time and after she left both nurses teased Kurt by saying he caught the most beautiful doctor in the medical school. This kind of news spread fast in the maxillofacial surgery community. Everybody in the department started to ask him questions about her. Over the weekend Kurt went to the community orchestra concert to watch Mia and her friends perform. Mia was a good cello player and performed from the heart.

After the concert, Kurt held Mia's hand and they started to aimlessly walk without knowing where to go. Finally, they found themselves at Kurt's apartment. Without saying a word, they started to kiss each other. Then they found themselves in bed making love. Now their bodies were giving them direction. They made love until morning. They didn't sleep, they just looked at each other, touching each other and enjoying the time they had together. After that night their relationship started to move on a fast track. Kurt was playing classical guitar now. He started to play Rodrigo's guitar concerto with the community orchestra musicians as a guest musician. Kurt and Mia spent time together, both at the hospital and in community concert hall. Kurt was falling in love with her. Mia was finishing her residency end of the semester, but Kurt had one more year to go.

CHAPTER VIII

One day when they were practicing at the concert hall Kurt started to play "The Look of Love." After he finished, he pulled out a red rose and gave it to Mia. As she came close to kissing Kurt, Kurt kneeled and pulled out a small box from his pocket. He opened it up, revealing a diamond ring, and asked her "Will you marry me, Mia?"

She jumped on him, started to kiss him, and said, "Many times yes, yes, yes."

This was the first time Kurt felt love since losing his family. He couldn't believe that such a beautiful and intelligent woman like Mia was in love with him. This was the first time he had fallen in love. They quickly found a two-bedroom apartment and started preparing for the wedding. Mia's parents invited Kurt for dinner. They were very friendly and proud of their daughter. Mia was very elegant and skillful. She decorated their apartment beautifully and made it look artistic. She was a good cook as well. She had inherited her mother's cooking skills. Mia taught Kurt to ski and ice skate. Kurt's one regret was not having any communication with his animal friends.

Spring quickly approached and Mia was close to finishing her residency.

One day Professors Schrolle and Eskinci approached Kurt and praised his skills as a surgeon. They offered him an assistant professor position in the maxillofacial surgery department after completing his residency. Before accepting, Kurt told them he needed to talk with Mia and get her approval as well. They said, "Think about it and let us know as soon as possible." Kurt and Mia had planned to go back to the US and settle in California, and if they could manage it, in Los Angeles so they could get close Kurts's ranch in Tucson, Arizona. When they were sitting on the porch, Kurt told Mia about the academic job offer from the medical school. She didn't react the way Kurt was expecting her to. She turned to Kurt and said with a serious look on her face, "Before we met each other, I joined the Doctors Without Borders organization, and they asked me to go a small village along the Kenya-Somalia border this summer. They have a clinic there. I plan on traveling from Graz with two nurses. A surgeon and two nurses from Los Angeles will join us there." Kurt was surprised and quizzically looked at her face. It wasn't easy for him to understand her decision to go. First, the Kenya-Somalia border was very remote and in the wilderness. Secondly, the notorious Al-Shabaab terrorist organization was very active there. Obviously, it wasn't a safe place to go. Kurt admired Mia so much and she was throwing her life in danger to help people in need. She came close to the Kurt and said, "I am sure you would do what I am doing today." According to Mia, the clinic was in a safe zone, and so far, no incidents had taken place there.

Kurt without hesitation said, "I'll come with you, love. Sitting here and eating by myself every day is not for me." She was very happy to hear Kurt's decision. She came close and started to kiss him.

She said, "Right now there are two doctors, four nurses and Kenyan helpers working there." Kurt started to think about how grueling the travel there would be. He anticipated limitations in water, food, medicine and medical equipment there. He was also concerned that Mia had no idea about protection there. There were a lot of questions that still needed to be answered, but Mia probably didn't know the answers. Kurt knew they were enrolling in a dangerous adventure.

CHAPTER IX

Kurt wanted to get more detailed information from the Doctors Without Borders organization. They couldn't provide all the information necessary to answer all of Kurt's questions about clinics safety. Clinic funded by Doctors without borders organization, and they were providing water, food, medications, and equipment. Kurt new he had no chance to change Mia's mind. He called Schrolle and Eskinci and told them that he will decide for Academic position after coming back Graz from their volunteer job.Kurt was paired with Professor Scott Smit at Doctors Without Borders to perform surgeries together. They decided to leave their dog Junior with Mia's parents. Junior was a German shepherd. He was a smart and quite animal. Kurt and Junior had a very good relationship. They would go on runs and play together. Junior wouldn't be happy about staying with Mia's parents, but they were animal lovers, and he would be in good hands. Mia and Kurt wrapped up their financial obligations and appointments as their departure date neared. Mia's love for Kurt grew deeper. His protective decision to travel with Mia to Kenya gave Mia more confidence.

Kurt and Mia wanted to meet with the two nurses who would travel with them. They were in their early forties. Karla was working for the obstetrics and gynecology department; Ida was emergency medical nurse working for the emergency medical department. They were calm and good-looking women. They had been volunteering for five years for the organization. During the meeting, the Doctors Without Borders officer appointed Kurt to manage the clinic. Kurt, who had no previous experience, accepted the offer involuntarily. A week before departure, Kurt began to spend more time with Junior. Kurt talked to Junior about his plans for the Kenya tip, about the dangers of Al-Shabaab and the risk of viral infections. Junior smartly listened to him. Junior's intuition was strong, and he could sense a problem coming up. Two days before departure they arranged a party at the Beer Keller. They all had nice time before flying to Kenya.

CHAPTER X

The departure day to Nairobi, Kenya, arrived. They met up with Ida and Karla at the Graz airport. Their flight had two legs, first from Graz to Rome, and then from Rome to Nairobi. It was a long flight but being with Mia made the flight fun for Kurt. They talked about their future, and they still had no idea where they should settle when they returned. They decided to discuss this in two months when they got back to Graz. Mia knew Kurt's heart was in Los Angeles, CA, on the other hand Kurt was flexible, if Mia considers staying in Austria he would accept the job in maxillofacial surgery department to make Mia happy. They held hands throughout the flight. This was the first time they were traveling out of Austria. After landing in Nairobi's crowded airport, they boarded a domestic flight to Liboi. Liboi was a town along the Somalia border. The closest Somalian city to Liboi was Hosingau. These were sparsely populated areas. If one traveled more southeast, they would reach more green foliage and forested areas. The Al-Shabaab terrorist organization was very active on either side of the border. They waited for two hours to fly to Liboi. The flight was on a charter plane. After some turbulence, they landed in Liboi. The clinic translator and security guard, Abdul, was waiting for them at the airport. He rented a minibus to transport them to the clinic, which was at the northern suburbs of Liboi and deserted. They had purposely built the clinic close to Somalia's border to help them too. The border was open and unprotected because protection was almost impossible. The clinic staff did not ask what the nationality was of the patients who came for treatment. They were helping citizens on both sides of the border.

After getting off the minibus, they could see the disappointment in each other's eyes. The living conditions were much worse than they expected. Dr. Scott Smit, and nurses Suzy and Liz were not there yet. According to Abdul, they were expected to arrive in a couple of days. The clinic and staff houses were made of wood. They needed to leave the windows open to keep the rooms cool. Inside the building, the patient rooms were divided with white tin covered in fabric. The clinic was decorated simply and had two exam rooms, a staff lounge and an operating room. The remainder of the space was filled with twenty patient beds. Fifteen of them were occupied already. Abdul showed them the doctors' and nurses' house. The house had six rooms, and Abdul showed the largest room to Mia and Kurt. They were the only married couple there. There wasn't a bathroom in the building. There were two showers and two toilets outside of the building. Taking a shower requires that someone pour water on you.

All the water came from water tankers. It was necessary to boil the water before drinking it. Water was equivalent to gold in Liboi. The food was provided by the Doctors Without Borders organization, and they were mostly high protein vegetarian foods and snacks.

They had two local nurses and additional staff. After such a long trip they were all tired, and they decided to have a meeting when Scott and the nurses arrived. Kurt and Mia decided to have a shower before getting some rest. They poured water on top of each other for the shower. They were having fun and joking about it. They didn't have a sewage system and a whiff of feces wafted out from the restrooms. It reminded Kurt of when he and his father would camp for many days at a time and would use the outdoor toilets. Therefore, it was easy for Kurt to adapt to the restroom in Liboi but Mia had a harder time adjusting.

The next day Abdul went back to the Liboi airport to pick up Scott, Liz and Suzy. Abdul came back with them around evening time. They all looked very tired. After their arrival, everyone introduced themselves. The Austrian medical team spoke English so English became the first language there. According to the Doctors Without Borders organization's schedule, the previous doctors and nurses had left the clinic two days ago. For the last two days, the local nurses were taking care of the patients, and they weren't accepting new patients until the new medical team arrived.

After a short introductory meeting, they decided to meet again the following morning. Mia and Kurt decided to go out exploring. There wasn't a lot to see, as most of the buildings were surrounded by shrubs. Kurt was expecting to see some local animals such as cheetahs, baboons, zebras and possibly lions, but didn't have a chance to see most of them. He also didn't want to risk speaking with the animals, because if anybody, including Mia, saw him they would think he was a weirdo. Word of their arrival to the clinic spread to nearby villages, and patients started to come quickly. They didn't have enough equipment to address every case. While the Kenyan authorities had promised them a Kenyan doctor and equipment, there was no mention about it yet.

Kurt and Scott operated together. Scott was a good general surgeon, and Kurt learned a lot from him. In fact, within one month, Kurt learned quite a lot of general surgery and gynecology from Scott. Head and neck or maxillofacial surgeries were rare there.

CHAPTER XI

The citizens on both sides of the border were severely deprived and malnourished. Water was scarce and the villagers could only harvest hay. Unemployment was very high as well. Both governments had implemented plans to improve the conditions, but terrorism, corruption and lack of education were big obstacles. The area was tagged with high level alerts by the government for terrorism. On the other hand, there was intense foreign interest in the terrorist organizations. The biggest threats came from the Al-Shabaab terror organization, which was originally from Somalia. Kenyan security forces were pushing back at the Al-Shabaab terrorists from both sides of the border.

The locals were the eyes and ears for the Kenyan security forces. In turn, Al-Shabaab were following police activities and collecting money from locals on both sides of the border. Most foreign countries had a travel warning in the area. The roads were very poorly maintained, especially where the clinic was located. Traveling at night in the area was not recommended. Besides Al-Shabaab, there were religious, ethnic, land and livestock disputes that led to big problems in the area. The patients coming to the clinic were mostly dehydrated, malnourished and had injuries, broken bones, gastrointestinal problems and infections. This was in addition to the obstetric and gynecological problems that existed.

Female genital mutilation was another big problem. Scott was very busy dealing with orthopedic surgeries secondary to broken bones, and Kurt assisted him. As an internal medicine Dr Mia was accepting new patients, schwester Karla was a midwife, and she was delivering babies. One month had passed, and it was almost June. After a hard day's work, the staff would get together in the evenings. They would play volleyball or chess. The volleyball games consisted of USA versus Austria. Scott was the USA team captain, and Kurt was the Austrian team captain. The referee was Abdul, and the spectators were the other clinic workers and some locals. They had a lot of fun during the volleyball games. It was terrible having not enough water, and no shower after the games. After sunset, they read books, or they discussed their future while others played chess. They all had complete confidence in each other professionally. Kurt's calm, quiet, supportive and helpful manner made him a natural leader for the team. They took direction from Kurt without any question.

One night, while Kurt and Mia were on a walk, they started to talk about the academic job that was offered to Kurt in Graz before they left. They knew Mia could find a job easily in Graz as well. Again, they decided to have a decision after the volunteering job in Kenya was over.

CHAPTER XII

One hot summer night after dinner Kurt took his guitar out and started to sing some country songs. The last song he played was "Somalia" by Al Di Meola. Everybody started to look a little bit homesick by the end of his performance. Kurt and Mia sat down and looked up at the beautiful sky from where they were sitting. Mia came close to Kurt and put her hand on Kurt's shoulder and said, "I got you a gift." She gave him a local handmade baby figurine. Kurt looked at Mia's face in surprise. He suspected but he wanted to hear it from Mia, so he looked at her with demanding eyes. She kissed Kurt on his cheek and said, "I am pregnant." Kurt stood up and grabbed Mia, lifting her up into his arms. He kissed her. They both were very happy because they wanted to have a baby. They had been in love ever since they first knew each other. The baby was another proof of their love for each other. This was the best news Kurt heard since they came to Kenya.

After they calmed down, Kurt asked Mia, "How long have you known you were pregnant?" She said almost three months. Kurt suspected that Mia knew about the pregnancy before coming to Kenya and thought Kurt wouldn't let her go to Kenya if he knew about it. He always respected Mia. She had very high morals and ethics. Although she knew how dangerous this part of the world was, she valued her work in helping other people.

Kurt never alerted her or others on the medical team about the Al-Shabaab organization. He assumed they all knew the danger, but after hearing Mia's surprising pregnancy news which she didn't tell him pregnancy until they arrive clinic. Pregnancy news raised Kurt's fear. Anything could happen because the Kenyan troops were not close to them. Now they had three more weeks to go, and lots of sleepless nights were waiting Kurt. From now on, he had to protect not only his loving wife but their unborn child as well.

Kurt had nothing to protect them during an unexpected danger. They were defenseless at the clinic. During these sleepless nights, Kurt would wake up in the middle of the night and go out to listen to the howling coming from afar. He was listening to the animals and telling them about how defenseless they were, and about Mia's pregnancy. A couple of days later they shared Mia's pregnancy with the others. Everybody congratulated them, and hugged Mia. Kurt and Mia again began to plan their future. Should they raise their child in Graz, or should they move to California? The discussions were endless. If they have a girl, what kind of sports or instruments should she play? Same with a boy. Mia's and Kurt's conversations after the pregnancy news were almost always the same. Kurt's nightmares continued. He knew his nightmares would finally end when they left Kenya.

CHAPTER XIII

A week before flying back home, they were very busy in the clinic with patients, and they were all dreaming of a cold shower after the day was over. Then suddenly they heard several gunshots. An angry looking local was yelling outside. Kurt immediately cautioned everyone to lie down.

Kurt knew the gunshots were from an automatic weapon, probably an AK-47. Kurt had experience with weapons. His father taught him about weapons on their desert trips. Kurt never carried a gun, although there were no restrictions on carrying weapons openly in Arizona. Kurt stuck his head out a window. There were several local people outside, and they were carrying automatic weapons. They were yelling "Abdul!" possibly asking questions about the clinic.

Before going outside to talk to Abdul, Kurt turned to Mia, Scott and the others. "Please stay calm, don't move, don't do anything unnecessary. I'll go and talk with them."

Mia looked at Kurt with a pleading face and said, "Please don't go outside, please. Please don't do it."

Kurt turned to her and said, "I must. Keep everybody calm. Do not move under any circumstances. I love you and our child."

Kurt knew it wasn't a good situation, and probably would not end well. He turned to Dr. Scot Smit and told him, "Scott, please keep everybody together, don't move until I say otherwise." Scott comforted Kurt with a nod in agreement. Kurt started to walk out of the clinic with both of his hands up. As he passed through the door, two terrorists grabbed him through the door and brought him to the terrorist in charge. Abdul was standing there and the terrorist in charge was yelling at him. Kurt approached Abdul and asked, "Who are they and what do they want?"

"They are Al-Shabaab members, they are coming from Somalia, and they all loaded with heavy weapons. They are bloodthirsty terrorists, and they will kill everyone without any hesitation. They are asking for *hekim*, which means doctor, so they probably have some wounded terrorists somewhere," replied Abdul.

Abdul translated what the terrorist in charge said, "If hekim comes with us, we will not touch the others in the clinic." He then said, "They want me to go with hekim so I can translate."

Kurt said, "Okay, Abdul, if they don't touch anybody in the clinic, I'll go with them."

While Abdul was talking with the terrorists, Kurt looked back at Mia. The clinic staff were looking back at Kurt with fear. After the terrorist accepted the deal, Kurt went back to Mia and the others. He explained what would happen.

They all became very anxious, and told Kurt, "Please don't go."

Kurt told them again, "If I don't go, they will kill everybody in this clinic without any hesitations."

Mia approached Kurt, "Don't go, Kurt, please don't go."

Kurt said again, "Look, Mia, if I don't go, they will kill everybody including me. Please stay with everybody no matter what happens. Don't leave this clinic. I'll be back after I treat their injured fighters."

Mia looked at Kurt with fear and started to cry hysterically. She felt guilty that she was the reason they came here in the first place. Kurt had warned her many times about the dangers, but because of her pride and principles, Kurt had ended up in Kenya.

Kurt said goodbye to the others and shook their hands. He stopped in front of Dr. Scott, "Scott, after I leave, please take everybody to safety." He then hugged Mia and said, "Take care of yourself and our child."

Abdul came to the clinic and told Kurt, "They want to move right away." Abdul was very upset as well. He had a wife and children in Liboi. He didn't have an opportunity to say goodbye to them. Kurt and Abdul knew very well that they could be taken into captivity by the Al-Shabaab. It would likely not end well.

The clinic staff watched Kurt and Abdul leave with the terrorists from the clinic windows in astonishment. Kurt and Abdul knew they may not see their friends or loved ones again, and they both looked back one last time. When they got close, one of the terrorists tied a piece of cloth around Abdul's eyes and then hit him in the back of the head with the butt of his rifle. Kurt wanted to stop the guy by pushing him away but suddenly saw the other terrorist's rifles butt coming down on his head.

CHAPTER XIV

Kurt woke up in a dark cottage which only had one room. Kurt was lying on the floor with a bad headache. He looked around and realized he was alone. The last thing he remembered was getting hit with a rifle butt on his head. He stood up and looked out the door; there were two guards sitting outside. Their faces were full of hatred. He went back into the cottage. The cottage was round, and the top of it was covered with sticks and shrubs. The cottage only had two small open windows.

After a while Abdul came in. He said, "We probably departed Liboi right after they hit me and you with the rifle. Probably they carried you with a handmade stretcher. As far as I understand from their talk, we passed into Somalia, and went north. After three or four hours of travel, they stopped at this village. The villagers are likely Al-Shabaab sympathizers. The terrorists hid their weapons under their clothes to look like nomads."

Abdul reported seeing some camels in the village. The terrorists probably came from the north and left their camels at this village before raiding the clinic. The further north consisted of mainly deserted areas, and there were no known villages there. For Kurt, going further north would make it much more difficult, if not almost impossible, to escape from captivity. This was a death sentence for them. They couldn't run from the terrorists when they were in a deserted area. They would be found right away by their tracks.

According to Abdul, they always traveled at night, likely because it is cooler, and they can go unseen in the dark.

Kurt asked Abdul, "Did you see or hear from Mia and the others before we left the clinic?"

Abdul said, "First they blindfolded me then they hit me, and after they hit you." Kurt began to worry about Mia, their child, and the others they left at the clinic. He hoped the terrorists hadn't done anything to them.

Kurt asked Abdul, "Where do you think they are taking us?"

Abdul said, "I don't know where, but as far as I understand they are taking us to their base camp to treat several wounded fighters, who must be important to them." Kurt was hopeful that the Kenyan Special Forces would look for them following their abduction, but the terrorists were going deep into Somalia where the Kenyan Special Forces would have no authority to save them.

The terrorists would stop at villages that contained their sympathizers. These villagers would help the terrorists logistically and join them for their raids. The corruption and lack of security forces on either side of the border was a big advantage for Al-Shabaab. Before sundown, they gave Kurt and Abdul local clothing to wear. They were getting ready to walk again after sundown. Kurt counted fifteen terrorists and three camels. They were hiding their weapons under the loads on the camels' backs. Whenever Kurt found an opportunity, he would whisper into the camels' ears. Whenever the terrorists saw Kurt talking to the camels, they would hit him with their sticks. The sticks hurt Kurt badly, and when they hit Kurt, he would think of Mia and their unborn child. During their night walk they saw more animals roaming about, probably in search of water because of the drought. Possibly, global warming was in effect in these areas.

Nomads and locals had begun to migrate to where the water was. The terrorists gave Kurt and Abdul a very small amount water. Kurt knew that soon he would start to dehydrate. Before sunrise they stopped in a small sympathizer village. The terrorists would not speak to Kurt and Abdul, and just stared at them with hostility. Kurt was constantly contemplating how to escape from them, but it would be easy to catch them i the desert by following their tracks, plus Kurt and Abdul did not have any water to survive on their own. The terrorists knew very well that Kurt and Abdul couldn't afford to escape now, therefore they were not enforcing strict confinement on them.

Now that they were in the desert, the terrorists started to cut Kurt and Abdul's water allotment down. Kurt began experiencing more muscle cramps as he began to dehydrate. Their food allowance was very limited as well. They were given pita bread, some dried meat and a date. Kurt began to lose track of time and was unsure how many days had passed since they left the clinic. After a long night walking, they stopped at a larger village. They had started their journey with fifteen men and were now down to five because the terrorists were dropping their fighters off at sympathizer villages along the way.

CHAPTER XV

The village they arrived at had women and children. They were all sitting in front of their houses. Kurt assumed that this village was the terrorist organization's base. At the center of the village was a larger house, and a group of people were sitting in front of it. Kurt thought these people must be the organization's leaders. They were all smoking hookahs. If Kurt didn't know what these guys are doing, and how terrorized them in their camp, he would never think they were a terrorist organization member. They were like chameleons; after completing their terrorist activities, they became nomads and villagers. After some time passed, their leader called Kurt and Abdul to approach them. He talked to Abdul for a few minutes Abdul turned to Kurt, "One of their leaders and four fighters were wounded, probably during a terrorist raid. They urgently need surgery, and they are asking for you to operate on them. If any of them loses their life, punishment for you and I will be very severe." Kurt was expecting sooner or later that this would happen. Before they were taken captive, the terrorists were loudly yelling for "hekim" during their clinic raid. Kurt was reluctant to treat terrorists so they could go out and continue to kill people. On the other hand, he was a doctor. No matter who they were, he felt a moral obligation to treat them. He finally decided he would provide the minimal required medical care, such that they would live but couldn't resume terrorist activities again. He didn't know if he could do this, but he would try. After working with Scott, Kurt had become a very skilled general surgeon; he could even perform gynecological surgeries.

After listening to Abdul, Kurt became confused. He knew that unless a rescue operation by the Kenyan authorities took place, they would be held captive by terrorists for a long time; therefore, he knew they needed to cooperate with them. Kurt and Abdul were put in a small nomad house with two fighters standing guard outside.

When they were inside, Kurt told Abdul, "We can't escape from them until we reach an environment that allows us to. I will treat their wounded friends with a minimum intervention." Abdul nodded in agreement with Kurt. Abdul was also thinking about his wife and children every day. He was eager to escape from the terrorists as much as Kurt was.

A terrorist they previously saw sitting in front of the larger nomad house, possibly a leader, came into Kurt's and Abdul's house. He asked them to follow him using a hand gesture. He took them to the larger house. The house was dark and had six floor beds in it. Five of them were filled with their injured fighters. They were all in very poor condition. The leader asked Kurt to treat them. Kurt didn't know what kind of injuries they had. With Abdul's help, he examined each wounded fighter. He found that two had broken bones, one had an abdominal bullet injury, and the other two appeared to have infections secondary to abdominal injuries.

Abdul explained the injuries that Kurt uncovered to the leader and told him what surgical equipment, medications and blood they needed to treat them. They took Kurt into another smaller room and showed him their cache of medical equipment and medications. It was clear they had stolen this equipment and medication during their raids to have a store of supplies here. Kurt couldn't believe what he saw. They had almost everything that he needed. Kurt and Abdul started to work on the injured terrorists. It took them three days to finish treating them all. Kurt did the minimum required to keep them alive. After they were finished, the terrorists beat them with long wood sticks and pushed them back into their nomad house.

It was very difficult for them to stay strong psychologically and physically. They had nothing to read, and very little food and water. They were not allowed to take any baths and were beaten with sticks every day.

CHAPTER XVI

One evening while Kurt was dreaming of Mia and their child, the terrorists came into their house, and asked Kurt and Abdul to follow them. There were six terrorists with fully loaded weapons and hand grenades standing outside. Obviously, they were going on a raid somewhere. They made Kurt and Abdul walk toward the west all night long. Kurt's father, Joe, had taught him well how to determine his direction in the desert. They were in a hurry, probably because they were trying to pass into Kenya before sunrise. Right before sunrise, they reached a small village and stopped there to rest. The sympathizer villagers hugged the terrorists in greeting. They stayed there for two days. They filled their water bags and restocked their bags with food before they started to walk again. Two new terrorists with fully loaded weapons joined them from the village. After ten days, they stopped at another village to restock. They now had sixteen terrorists. Before sunrise, they stopped and surrounded a village.

Abdul came close and whispered to Kurt, "This is a Kenyan village."

They raided the village and abducted the children, killing the others. They also took all their valuables. They left Abdul and Kurt to watch while they raided the defenseless village. Kurt and Abdul watched in horror. Some of the villagers had rifles, but they were not automatic. They tried to resist the terrorists, but the well-equipped Al-Shabaab militants took control right away. They split children from their families and killed the other villagers in cold blood. It was a gruesome scene for Kurt and Abdul. One of the terrorist fighters was shot very badly by the villagers. Two terrorists brought him to Kurt and Abdul. They asked Kurt to treat their friends.

Kurt told them, "I can't help him here; he needs surgery." They immediately prepared a stretcher and carried him back east. Before sunrise they reached their friendly village again. They asked Kurt to operate on their friends there. After examining the wounded guy, Kurt told Abdul, "The bullet made a hole in his intestines and is lodged in there. It's very difficult to operate and save him. He has an infection and has lost a lot of blood."

Kurt only cleaned the exterior of the wound and bandaged it. He said to Abdul, "He may live one or two more hours." Kurt was right because after an hour or so the terrorist died. The other fighters began to look at Kurt and Abdul with animosity. Kurt knew what would happen to them, but he didn't know when and where. They had two boys and five girls captive with them. The following evening, they started to walk again. They stopped at sympathizer villages, dropping off fighters and captives along the way. They were selling their captives to the villagers. They reached their main village with one less terrorist. They put Kurt and Abdul back into their nomad house with two terrorists standing guard outside. After some time passed, four terrorists came and pushed Kurt and Abdul toward the village center. At the center of the village stood their leader, who was giving a speech to the villagers in a high volume with an inspiring tone. Abdul starts to look with fear at Kurt. Abdul understood what the leader was saying. The terrorists came and ripped open Kurt's and Abdul's shirts to expose their upper bodies.

There were two large poles in the middle of the village. The terrorists pushed Kurt and Abdul against the poles and tied them by their hands, so their faces were against the poles and their backs were exposed to the village. All the villagers gathered around them with excitement. Kurt and Abdul figured out their punishment right away. Two Al-Shabaab terrorists with their long sticks approached Kurt and Abdul. At that moment Kurt thought about Mia and their child and began to make plans for their future for when he got back to Graz. He was hoping that dreaming about his family would prevent him from feeling the pain. Suddenly the stick hit his back and continued hitting him without interruption. The stick was hitting him harder and harder, but his dreams of his family started to disappear because it was impossible for Kurt to stay conscious. The pain took this mind from Mia and their child and submerged him into the darkness of unconsciousness and oblivion.

CHAPTER XVII

Kurt opened his eyes and was in unbearable pain. He had no idea how many hours or days had passed. Now pain was keeping his entire body hostage. He wasn't unable to think, and he couldn't touch any part of his body. Blood was everywhere. After a while he looked around for Abdul and saw that he was laying on the other side of the nomad house. He could hear Abdul's moaning. Obviously, he was in the same situation. He examined Abdul's body from where he was laying. Abdul's entire body was covered with blood, and his upper body was full of fresh cuts. Kurt assumed his back was in the same condition. They didn't have a mirror, but Kurt assumed the same thing happened to his body.

While they were torturing them, the terrorists were expecting Kurt and Abdul to cry out for forgiveness, but neither Kurt nor Abdul gave them this pleasure. Kurt had a reason to stay alive; he was in love with Mia. She was the only one person he had in this world. Her love was giving Kurt the strength to stay alive.

The terrorists didn't give them extra water to wash their wounds. Abdul asked for some painkillers from them, but to no avail. When they were able to stand again, they started to clean their wounds with their daily water allotments.

After this horrific incident they totally lost a sense of time. Now they didn't know the time, days, months, but they were estimating seasons. One day they saw Al-Shabaab terrorists getting ready for another bloody raid. They didn't bring Kurt and Abdul with them this time. Kurt and Abdul were happy not to have to go with them. They did not have to watch their bloody attacks on the innocent. They also had some time to recuperate. Approximately two weeks later, the terrorists came back with two injured fighters. One had a leg injury, and the other had an abdominal injury. Most of the terrorists waited outside of their medical clinic and gave Kurt and Abdul evil looks to remind them of the consequences if any death took place.

Kurt removed the bullet from the injured leg, cleaned up the wound and sutured it closed. There were likely broken bone fragments inside the wound, but Kurt had no choice but to leave the bone as it was under their current environment. The second injury was very bad. The bullet had ripped a segment of the intestine open and settled down close to the liver, risking rupture to the liver capsule and death by hemorrhage. Kurt was finally able to remove bullet after operating for a long time, but the chance of survival for the terrorist was still slim. Kurt explained the situation to Abdul. Abdul translated Kurt's words to their leader. They were all looking at Kurt and Abdul in fury. After two days of struggling, the terrorist died. Kurt and Abdul were ready for the consequences. The terrorists didn't waste much time. They grabbed Kurt and Abdul, took them to the center of the village and beat them again in front of an audience. Every villager was very happy to see Kurt and Abdul suffer.

They were bloody, heartless terrorists. They were abducting children from villagers, they were killing others in the villages, then they were raping the children and selling them to their sympathizers. Their actions were disgusting and unforgiveable.

After a very long period, they decided to go raid again. They were probably going to take Kurt and Abdul with them again. Kurt had tremendous pain from his wounds. He could barely stand up and walk. During these trips out of the camp, Kurt was always trying to figure out a way to escape. He knew that they needed more dense foliage and forests to escape from the terrorists, otherwise they could catch them very easily by tracing their tracks. During the raids, the terrorists would always leave only one heavily armed guard with them. Currently they were hiding north in a deserted part of Somalia. Kurt knew his plan would only work in southern Somalia along the Kenyan border. This area was forested and full of wild animals.

Most of the time, the terrorists didn't have bad injuries so there were no punishments for Kurt and Abdul. Kurt's and Abdul's wounds started to heal, but both of their upper bodies were full of scars that looked ugly and painful. They were both skinny and pale now. Their muscles were okay because of the long walks with the terrorists. They would need their muscles to escape. They both had long beards, and they were beginning to look like nomads.

One day Kurt decided to explain his escape plan to Abdul. He said, "My plan is not very sophisticated. If we reach dense foliage and a forested area, we will subdue the guard while the terrorists are on their raid, then we will get his water and food. We will then run through the forest to the Kenyan border. If we run through with the animals, they can't trace us." They both were ready to run away from the terrorists, and they had no more strength and patience to stay with them. They both had families, and very much missed them. They knew if they were caught trying to escape, the punishment would be execution. If they stayed, they would kill them one day anyway so dying while escaping from them would be a much more honorable death.

CHAPTER XVIII

Kurt and Abdul were waiting now with hope. Days, weeks and months passed without a chance to escape. Kurt guessed that they had been in captivity for at least two and half or three years.

Kurt would frequently dream of Mia and their child. Their child would now be two years old. Kurt had developed a lot of wounds, both emotionally and physically, but he knew they would all heal once he got back to his family. He dreamt of settling down in Los Angeles, and spend some time close ocean. He knew they would both find jobs easily there. They could go to the ranch in Tucson where they could horseback ride and hike whenever they wanted. For now, it was all a dream.

Escaping the Al-Shabaab terrorists was the primary topic of discussion between Kurt and Abdul. One evening they took Kurt and Abdul from their captive nomad house on a bloody raid again. This time their fighters were very heavily armed. They had two camels with them. The camels were loaded with water, food and ammunition. They were walking as before, stopping at sympathizer villages along the way. This time they were adding more fighters than before, and they were walking south.

Kurt couldn't believe they were finally heading south; he had been waiting for this to happen for a long time. Kurt knew from the surrounding environment where they were now and that to reach the south would take a long time. The further south they walked, the more crowded they became. According to Abdul they were going to raid the Kenyan government troops.

Kurt and Abdul knew this would be their one and only chance to escape. They were ready to escape, whatever the cost. They would rather die trying to escape, even though their chance of freedom was slim. They felt like they were dying every day during their captivity.

Days into their walk south, the environment started to change. The foliage became denser, and trees began to appear; Kurt was so happy to see plants around them. One day when they were camped in the forest, three of the fighters left the camp; they were obviously going to reconnaissance. Terrorists must have been close to their targets; possibly they were waiting to raid their target at the right time. Some of the terrorists were wearing suicide vests to blast.Kurt and Abdul considered every option to escape, and they were assuming that the raid would be very bloody after seeing suicide west carrying terrorists. Abdul overheard their conversations and said, "They will raid against the Kenyan troops inside the Kenyan border." A day later, the fighters returned to the camp.

The terrorists sat in a circle and began a discussion in high volume. According to Abdul, they had decided to raid the Kenyan troops early in the morning before sunrise. Kurt and Abdul were getting ready to escape while the terrorists were getting ready to raid. Kurt and Abdul had their best sleep that night ever since they had been captured by the terrorists.

CHAPTER XIX

The terrorists, Kurt and Abdul woke up early in the morning to prepare for the raid. The terrorists had confidence now that Kurt and Abdul wouldn't try to escape; therefore, they left one terrorist to watch them. Kurt and Abdul's plan was very simple; they would wait until they heard the terrorists' weapons firing, then Kurt would talk to their guard like he talked to the animals. After catching the guard's attention, Abdul would subdue him. Then they would run as fast as they could.

They heard the weapons fire and grenades go off; it was time for Kurt and Abdul to escape. Kurt talked to the terrorist like he talked to the animals; the terrorist was startled and looked at Kurt with one eye open. Kurt was successful in getting his attention. Abdul grabbed a rock and jumped over the guard and hit him hard across the head. They didn't know if the guard was dead or alive; they didn't care anyway. They grabbed water, food and weapons from the guard, then hid him a little further from the camp underneath some large plants.

This was the time to run to freedom and to their loved ones. They were running southwest to Kenya. The foliage was very dense, and it was slowing them down. They stopped from time to time to take a small break and sip some water, then they would run again. After a while their speed started to slow down. By the afternoon, the foliage started to thin out; Kurt and Abdul ran fast again, because now they were more visible and were open targets. They knew the terrorists were looking for them by now. Kurt told Abdul to run through the animals tracks so they could throw the terrorists off their trail. They were taking shorter breaks now and breathing heavily.

Running away from the terrorists became harder and harder for them. They had very limited water left. They were getting tired and slowing down. They were desperately looking for the sun to set so they could hide somewhere and rest. They dreamt of a safe shelter like an oasis in the desert. They suddenly heard gunshots from an automatic weapon. The terrorists had finally found them. Kurt and Abdul started to run again. They didn't know how many terrorists were following them, but Kurt and Abdul knew they were faster runners. Kurt and Abdul had no chance to hide now. They were running as fast as they could. The automatic weapon sounds were getting closer and closer.

Suddenly Kurt felt a burn on the left side of his abdomen. He touched the spot with his hand and saw blood. He didn't know how bad the injury was. He yelled out to Abdul, "They shot me in the abdomen. I can't run anymore. We must either separate or hide somewhere." They slowed down a little bit to wrap the wound with a piece of cloth. They knew they would never surrender to the terrorists again. Kurt told Abdul, "You don't have to wait for me. Run!"

Abdul objected to leaving him alone. He said, "First we need to find shelter for you, then I'll run again to find help." Finding shelter would be a miracle for them now.

Kurt saw a zebra herd coming toward them and told Abdul, "Follow me." They started to run toward the zebras. Kurt was yelled out at the zebras to help hide them. As they got closer to the zebras, the zebra herd formed a crescent shape. Kurt and Abdul ran into the middle of the crescent and the zebras closed the crescent around them and took their herd shape again. They were walking slowly so Kurt and Abdul could adjust their tempo to theirs. This was either a miracle or thanks to Kurt's ability to communicate with animals.

Kurt couldn't run anymore; he was losing a lot of blood and he was tired. The zebras halted their movement to sleep for the night. They no longer heard the terrorists. The terrorists would never think that Kurt and Abdul were hiding in a zebra herd. Kurt asked Abdul to run and find help now that it was dark.

Abdul looked at Kurt hesitantly, and said, "I'll find help and I'll be back, my friend." Abdul hugged Kurt; his eyes were wet, and Kurt saw Abdul cry for the first time. They had always supported each other during their captivity. Now they had to separate to stay alive even though there was a small chance of surviving. Abdul started to run again to West Kenya, and Kurt was alone now. He lay down in the middle of the zebra herd. He knew there wasn't much time: he was losing blood quickly. If Abdul didn't show up before sunrise, either he would die, or the terrorists would catch and kill him. He dreamt of Mia and their child. He thought about how thankful he was for Mia's love. He began to lose consciousness.

CHAPTER XX

Abdul was running full speed after leaving the zebra herd; he was running to save Kurt's life. He knew he had very little chance of saving him, but it was still worth it to try. Kurt's life depended on it. Abdul wasn't running just to save Kurt; he was running to get his freedom back and to see his family again. Abdul saw lights from a distance near the edge of the forest. Abdul turned his direction toward the lights, which became clearer as he got close. Abdul began to pray as he ran toward the light, "God, please show me the Kenyan troops." He saw a Kenyan troop camp when he approached and noted that they were Kenyan Special Forces. He yelled out for help. They ran up to Abdul, and Abdul identified himself to them. They looked at him with suspicion and took him to their captain. Abdul didn't waste time in telling the captain who he was, and what happened to Kurt, describing his injury to him.

According to the captain, they were looking for the Al-Shabaab terrorist group after yesterday's raid on their border patrol. The terrorists had killed fifteen Kenyan troops yesterday. The captain asked that four of his best soldiers get ready to rescue Kurt, and at the same time he asked for a chopper from their base to evacuate Kurt to a hospital. He said over the radio, "I'll give you coordinates after we reach the wounded person."

The captain, four of his troops and Abdul stepped into an armored vehicle that they navigated based on Abdul's directions. Abdul was praying that Kurt was okay. He told the captain they were very close to the target around 2 a.m.. The captain called for the chopper, which was already airborne, and gave the pilots the coordinates of their location.

The pilots told them, "We will be there in twenty minutes."

Abdul warned the captain, "We are very close to the area I left him."

The captain asked the driver to turn on all their headlights and for everyone to keep a lookout for terrorists. They didn't see any terrorists around after checking, and the captain called the chopper pilot and asked them to comb through the area to see if there were any terrorists still around.

After conformation from the chopper pilot, they got out of the armored vehicle, and started to walk toward the zebras. The zebras were still there grazing, and they were holding the same shape that Abdul had left them in. Once they got close to the zebras, they opened a passageway for Abdul and the captain, who ran to the middle of the herd. They found Kurt lying there unconscious. The captain asked for the four soldiers to keep a parameter and the zebras left. The captain asked the chopper to land in the area where they were signaling with their lights. Abdul tried to wake Kurt, but he wasn't successful. Kurt had lost so much blood that he couldn't keep consciousness. The chopper landed and two medical soldiers jumped out and ran to them with a stretcher. They carefully put Kurt on the stretcher and carried him to the chopper. They were not wasting any time; they understood the urgency right away. The captain allowed Abdul to get on the chopper and they were airborne right away. The medical soldiers started to give Kurt IV fluids for the hemorrhage. After forty-five minutes, they arrived at the military hospital.

CHAPTER XXI

At the military hospital they took Kurt immediately into emergency surgery. After a couple of hours, the doctor came out to talk to Abdul. "He was lucky. The bullet entered from the left side of the abdomen and didn't harm any intestines or the spleen before exiting from his back, but Mr. West lost a significant amount of blood and may be infected. We will give him five units of blood product and start antibiotics. He is very fragile right now. As far as I can see, he must be a tough person. Hopefully he will come back soon."

After talking with the doctor, Abdul called his family. He was crying while he was talking with them; he explained briefly how they escaped, and how he was at the hospital waiting for Kurt to recover. He told them, "Once Dr. Kurt regains his consciousness, I will come home."

Three days later, Kurt opened his eyes and saw Abdul. Abdul hugged Kurt and they thanked each other. They knew they would not see each other again, not because they didn't want to, but because they didn't want to remember the almost three years of torture and pain endured at the hands of the terrorists. Tears were welling up in Abdul's eyes as he stood up and saluted Kurt one last time before walking out of the room. Suddenly Kurt felt very alone and fell asleep.

A week later, they transferred Kurt to another military hospital in Nairobi. While at the hospital, a US diplomat, an Austrian diplomat, and a Doctors Without Borders clinic member visited Kurt. They asked him if he needed anything; they would be very happy to help him. Kurt asked all of them to communicate with his family. They all promised to create a connection with them as soon as possible. All three of them told him the same thing, "We don't want your escape and freedom to be public before you leave Nairobi. We don't know how Al-Shabaab will react to this news."

Kurt didn't respond. He had no strength and power to do otherwise. He didn't want to confront the media anyway. According to the Doctors Without Borders clinic member, they had relocated Abdul and his family to a hospital in Nairobi and gave them new identification cards. This news was a big relief for Kurt. He knew the terrorists would follow Abdul and his family if they stayed in Liboi.

Kurt still had no idea about Mia and their child. It was close to Christmas and all he wanted was to see them. He knew he was very weak physically and emotionally but seeing them would certainly be a remedy for him. After another week passed, Kurt met with the Doctors Without Borders clinic members again. He learned that after the terrorist raid on the clinic, they had closed the clinic permanently and sent all the patients to surrounding local hospitals. He had no information about what happened to the other foreign workers and doctors. The Kenyan army invaded the terrorist camp and terminated the Al-Shabaab members.

CHAPTER XXII

Now Kurt was ready to fly to Graz, Austria, to see his loved ones. The flight from Nairobi was almost seventeen hours long and involved a couple of connections to get to Graz. Kurt was still very weak and slept for most of the time. He was sleeping in peace now that there was no terrorist threat and fear of torture. He arrived in Graz in the evening. He passed quickly through passport control and walked through the exit to baggage claim. He was searching for Mia and their child, but he didn't see them. He waited a little bit at baggage claim, and he finally saw Mia's parents, Martha, and Bernard Kraus. They looked at him with sadness and devastation. Kurt's stomach dropped when he saw their faces. He slowly walked toward them. He was trying to think positively, and he was murmuring to himself, "Probably they were very busy and could not come to the airport to see me."

When he approached Martha and Bernard, he saw that their eyes were full of tears. Kurt began to shake, and said, "What is wrong?"

Martha and Bernard hugged Kurt, then they started to cry hysterically. Kurt was flabbergasted and was waiting for some explanation. They didn't say a word. They grabbed Kurt's hands and walked with him into a guest room, and they sat down. Bernard started to talk. "After the terrorists hit you with the weapon, Mia started to run toward you. One of the terrorists immediately shot her. Dr Scott and the others tried to save Mia and the fetus, but she passed instantaneously."

Kurt started to moan, "It's all my fault. I shouldn't have left her alone."

Kurt couldn't hear anything, and he didn't want to hear anyway. He had stayed alive in captivity for Mia and their child. If he knew they were dead, he wouldn't have had a reason to stay alive. He started to feel very lonely. Mia was everything to him. They were planning to settle down in California, which they both could find job easily, and they were dreaming of horseback riding, hiking at Kurt's ranch in Tucson. They were all gone now, and Kurt suddenly felt like he was falling into a deep hole. He just wanted to cry, but he forgot how to cry after his captivity. There was nothing left but deep sorrow.

Kurt felt someone shaking him. It was Bernard. "Kurt, you are not responsible for my daughter's death. You surrendered to the terrorists voluntarily, and you saved all the others. You are a hero. They all said the same thing. Neither you nor my daughter are to be blamed. If there is anyone to blame, it's the terrorists."

Kurt looked into their eyes but couldn't talk. If he knew this would happen, he wouldn't have left her alone. Martha and Bernard were very noble people; they accepted their daughter's loss although it was difficult. They were still crying. They hugged Kurt but Kurt was frozen. They stood holding each other for some time, then Martha grabbed Kurt's hand and they walked out of the airport. They drove Kurt to their home. Once they opened the door, Junior jumped on Kurt and started to lick his face. This was another very emotional confrontation for Kurt.

Martha took Kurt to the second floor where Mia's room was. They kept the room the same as it was before Mia left the house to marry Kurt. She said, "Kurt, you can stay in this room if you want. We lost our daughter, but you are our son, and you are still alive and here." She left the room quietly and closed the door.

Kurt started to look at the walls. Mia's and Kurt's pictures were everywhere. Kurt looked at every picture with focused attention. She was so beautiful, so kind, so compassionate, and she was a good doctor and a very good musician. All these pictures reflected her skills and personality. Kurt's memory of her was flooded with their first meeting, his failure squeezing the ketchup bottle, their second meeting with the empty glass ketchup bottle, practicing music together, hiking, skiing and ice skating. The memories lived in the pictures on the walls. When Mia was living with her parents, she decorated her room beautifully. Kurt sat in the chair all night long. He couldn't sleep or touch anything. He refreshed his memory by looking at the pictures again and again. She was gone forever, but she would live in this room and in Kurt's memory. He should never have accepted this volunteer job, and he should have fought to not go to Kenya.

CHAPTER XXIII

After sunrise, Kurt took Junior for a walk. Junior was waiting for Kurt at the door. He was always happy to walk with Kurt. Kurt and Junior took a long walk and then went back to Martha's and Bernard's house. Martha and Bernard were waiting for them for breakfast.

Kurt didn't want breakfast and asked them, "Can you please take me to Mia's grave?"

They took him to the cemetery. Mia's grave was built from marble, and well taken care of. Kurt asked them, "Can you please leave me here for a while? I'll be back tonight." Kurt sat down by Mia's grave and told her what happened after the terrorists separated them. He told her every detail of his captivity and escape. He sat there talking, not looking around, and didn't notice when the sun started to set. Kurt eventually went back to Mia's parents' house. He told them, "I'll find a hotel tomorrow and stay there until I decide what to do." He found a guest house close to the hospital. He couldn't sleep at night. He kept blaming himself for Mia's and their child's death.

After a week, he decided to visit the maxillofacial surgery department. He called Dr. Shrolle and told him, "I would like to visit the clinic if it's okay with you." The following day he walked into the clinic. The minute he entered the clinic, the doctors and nurses began to applaud him. He was thinking that he didn't deserve a heroic greeting like this. He thought of himself as a coward. He left his wife alone at the hands of terrorists.

Shrolle and Eskinci came and shook his hand then they both hugged him. They didn't talk to him about the past because they figured from the way Kurt looked that it wasn't a topic he wanted to discuss. They asked him to reconsider their assistant professorship offer. Kurt politely told them, "After this tragic incident, it's best for me move back to the United States. I am thinking of moving back to Tucson and taking over the family ranch."

They both smiled and said, "We wish you the best." Then they give Kurt an envelope from Professor Scott Smit. Kurt opened the envelope after he left the maxillofacial surgery department.

"Dear Dr. Kurt West, we are very happy to hear that you are alive, but we are very sorry for Mia's tragic loss. My wife, my children, the other nurses, Liz and Suzy, their families, and myself are all grateful to you. You saved our lives. Please call us as soon as possible. Don't forget from now on we are your family. Prof Scott Smit."

Three days later, Kurt called Scott. "Hi Professor Smit,, this is Kurt West."

Scott said, "Please don't call me Professor Prof Smit. We are friends. Forget the formalities when talking to me."

Kurt didn't say anything and just smiled. Scott started to talk again, "Kurt, we need an assistant surgeon in our surgery department. I am the director of surgery department at the University of California, Los Angeles. I want to add a maxillofacial surgeon to our department. If you accept the position, you will work with me in general surgery as well. You were the best surgeon I've worked with."

Kurt said, "Thank you very much for the offer, and I'll get back to you in a few days."

CHAPTER XXIV

Kurt thought about the offer after hanging up the phone. He had wanted to go back to Tucson before this offer. He wanted to live on the ranch but also needed a salary. He anticipated that the salary in Los Angeles would be high. He could fulfill his and Mia's dreams in Los Angeles. Three days later Kurt called Scott, and told him, "Once again, thank you very much for your kind offer. I was thinking of moving back to Tucson, but Mia's and my dreams were to move to California. You are helping our dream come true, and I accept your offer. It is an honor to work with you."

Scott said, "We thank you for accepting our offer. It's an honor work to work with such a great surgeon. But now you are both a great surgeon and a hero. I'll send you all the paperwork electronically right away. Please fill it out and send it back to us. Whenever you inform us of your flight dates, we will send you your flight tickets. I'll rent a condo for you that is close to the hospital, and you can stay there for as long as you want. We will talk about the details shortly."

Kurt wanted to stay in Graz for one more week to say goodbye to the maxillofacial surgery department and to Mia's parents. First, he called Mia's parents and told them, "Martha, I am going back to the United States next week. I'll settle in Los Angeles and work there. This was Mia's and my dream, and I am sure she is smiling down at me. If you don't mind, I'll take Junior with me, and I'll come to visit you tomorrow."

Martha began to cry, and said, "I am very happy to hear both of your dreams coming true. Junior is your dog. Of course, you can take him with you. He loves you anyway. If you need anything else or want to take something from Mia's room, let me know."

Kurt knew she was crying after hanging up the phone. He called Shrolle and Eskinci next and told them about his new job in California. He asked them if he could visit the clinic for a final farewell.

They told him they would arrange for a farewell party. "You can visit the clinic any time you want Kurt."

CHAPTER XXV

The next morning, he woke up very early and bought a dozen pink roses which he took to the cemetery. He sat down near Mia's grave for nearly the entire day and told her about his move to California. The following day he went to Martha and Bernard's house. They prepared a beautiful breakfast. They asked about Kurt's new job, and whatever they heard from Kurt made them happy. The final farewell came, and Kurt hugged them both. They were crying. He grabbed Junior and walked out of the door. He knew Mia's parents would never be the same again, just like him. They had all lost their main reason to live in this world.

Kurt walked for a while with Junior, then he left him at the guesthouse where he was staying. He took his guitar and walked to the music academy. He found his guitar teacher, then without a word they sat down and started to play Rodrigo's Guitar concerto.

The following day he walked to the clinic at the university hospital. They had a surprise clinic party for Kurt. Shwester Betty and Shwester Elisabeth were there. They both hugged Kurt; they both were crying and said, "We will never forget what you did. You are our hero."

Kurt smiled and kissed them both on the cheek. Everybody was discussing Kurt's Los Angeles job. They all were eager to visit him in California. Before Kurt left, they gave him a Graz-made guitar which was engraved with "Dr. Kurt West, Maxillofacial Surgeon, Graz, Austria." This gift was a big surprise for him, and he loved it. He personally shook everyone's hand and said goodbye to them. That evening they had another party at a local brewery, established in 1495. Kurt had his new guitar with him. He played them country songs from famous country stars as well as his own music.

The next day he took Junior on an early morning walk. They visited Junior's veterinarian afterwards. His paperwork was completed. He left Junior at the guesthouse and went to visit Mia's grave one last time. He stayed there all day again and told her what had happened since his last visit. He promised to visit again as soon as possible upon his return from Los Angeles.

CHAPTER XXVI

Kurt and Junior went to the airport early for Junior's airport screening. Kurt had first class tickets on Austrian Airlines, and they accepted Junior in the cabin. Their seat was large and there was a lot of leg space so Junior could sleep there during the long thirteen-hour flight. They slept for most of the flight. When they arrived in Los Angeles, Kurt got off the plane quickly to take Junior to the airport pet rest area. When they got to the airport exit, there was a surprise waiting for them. Scott and his family, and nurses Suzy and Liz with their families were all there waiting for him. The minute they saw Kurt, they all started to applaud him. Kurt and Junior were surprised. Kurt didn't know what to do.

They all came up to him one by one and introduced themselves, and said, "We are very sorry for your loss, and thank you very much for sending our parents back alive back."

Kurt didn't know what to do, he just shook everyone's hand and said, "Pleasure to meet you," in return.

Scott said, "I'll drop you off at your new home and then we will see you at the welcome party tonight."

Kurt and Junior's new home was very close to the university, and it had a small backyard. Kurt liked the house, especially the backyard. It would be a lifesaver for Junior. Kurt took a shower, took

Junior on a walk and then rested before he walked to the restaurant where the party was. It was a beautiful country style restaurant and bar. They probably picked this restaurant to remind him of Tucson. Kurt's dress code was country anyway. It was a very cordial meeting. They drank beer and conversed with each other. Some of them asked Kurt about his last name, and Kurt explained what his father use to do and how his name came from there. Scott approached Kurt with a guitar and asked him to play country music. Kurt knew this would happen and he was ready. He played famous country songs and his own songs. Everyone began to dance. This was a good start in Los Angeles for Kurt.

CHAPTER XXVII

Kurt woke up early Monday morning and prepared to go to the university hospital. Scott Smit was waiting for Kurt at the surgery department. They took a tour of the surgery department. Scott introduced Kurt to everybody. They were all nice and polite people. Kurt liked what he saw. They were fully equipped and staffed, and they were very busy. They didn't have a maxillofacial division yet. Scott's expectation was for Kurt to establish a maxillo-facial surgery division. Scott said to Kurt, "I'd like to work with you on surgeries like we were doing in Kenya. Working together, we can shorten operative time dramatically."

Kurt said, "It's a pleasure to work with you, Scott."

Kurt had his first operation with Scott the following day. The days started to follow each other and got busier and busier. Kurt never complained about working so much. In fact, working long hours kept him busy. He had no time to think about Somalia. He got home late, and Junior wasn't happy with that. Finally, Kurt hired a dog walker for Junior. He was a nice young man, and a dog lover. Obviously Junior liked him; he was happy whenever he saw him. Two months later, Kurt decided to buy a house. He wanted a one-bedroom studio with a car garage and a small patio for Junior.

Los Angeles home prices were very high, but Kurt had some money piled up in his bank account thanks to the Tucson ranch rent, so he was able to pay for a down payment and buy a

house. He found a well taken care of place in Santa Monica and bought it. Before he moved into the new house, he bought a Ford Raptor truck for weekend getaways. Kurt decorated his new house plainly. He did not have much furniture and decorations, but this left more space for himself and Junior.

The surgery department was very busy, and the other surgeons began to gain more confidence in him as they worked with him. Although he was a lonely cowboy, his relationship with his patients was very good. The staff were all happy with Kurt's care of patients. Over the weeks and months, respect, and admiration for him grew, and he became the second-best surgeon after Scott.

He never attended happy hours or weekend activities with the clinic personnel, doctors or students. He was still blaming himself for the loss of Mia and their child, and he never wanted to forget them. Scott was aware of this situation. He didn't want to talk about this incident with Kurt again. Talking would open the wounds again. Scott knew that in the long run Kurt's emotional, psychological wounds would never heal, but the external wounds have chance to heal except scars from tortures.

CHAPTER XXVIII

After a two-month stay in the condo rented by Scott, Kurt moved into his new house in Santa Monica. His new neighborhood was close to the beach. He started to take Junior on beachside walks. Junior loved this; he enjoyed that there were more people on the boardwalk, and more dogs were paying attention to him. Junior had never seen so many dogs walking around before. Kurt began to play guitar after work. Every time he sat down to practice, he remembered practicing with Mia.

After completely settling in the new house, Kurt made plans for his weekends off. He bought camping materials for himself and Junior and planned where they could camp far away from the public eye. He was particularly looking for deserted areas and hoped to see desert animals so he could talk to them. He wanted to talk to them about what happened when he was overseas.

During his first available weekend, he loaded his Raptor and drove to the Yuma desert. He found a nice campsite far from the dune-racing people. Almost every evening, Kurt sat down in his camping chair to observe the beautiful sky. It was so clear, like the Somalia desert; you could see every star. Junior listened to the howling desert animals with all his attention. Kurt took off his T-shirt; he never showed anybody the scars on his chest and back. He didn't want anyone to feel pity for him. He talked to the animals that were howling at him. He told them about his stay in Graz, Austria, and how he met Mia. He talked through everything in detail. A couple of hours before sunrise, the animals' howls dissipated, and Kurt decided to get some sleep.

After sunrise, Kurt and Junior took a run in the sand. It wasn't easy. Afterwards, Kurt assembled a tent for shade and played the guitar. In the evening he drove back to Los Angeles. While he was unloading his truck, he got an emergency phone call from the university hospital. The minute he got to the hospital; they briefed him about the emergency operation. "It was a traffic accident, and Scott is the primary surgeon. He asked for you personally." They began the operation together.

Days, weeks, and months passed like that, and Kurt was a lonely man again after Mia's loss.

On another weekend off he drove with Junior to the El Centro desert. The area was full of wildlife. Kurt specifically picked this area because it was rich with Big Horn sheep. Kurt camped at a remote area of the Yuka desert. This time he had experience from his last trip; he brought everything that was necessarily make their trip comfortable such as food and drink for him and Junior, and necessary tools for camping. After preparing his tent, he sat down with Junior to watch the star show. Kurt then prepared dinner at the campfire. The howling started after the campfire began to dim.

Kurt talked to the animals and told them about his trip to Kenya and Somalia in detail. Kurt and Junior saw animals hiding in the shade from afar. Kurt didn't know if they were listening to him, but he told his story anyway. The animals were good listeners. They did not feel any pity and they did not gossip. These trips became

Kurt's way to relax and were therapeutic. They helped Kurt feel better for a while.

His colleagues at the medical school and hospital invited Kurt to their parties and dinners. They were all nice coworkers, but Kurt didn't want to form close relationships with anybody. He was still mourning the loss of Mia and their child. He had no intention of getting together with anyone, or of falling in love again. He knew he couldn't afford another loss. Kurt was a hero to those who knew about his story. Kurt never thought about himself like that; he thought he was a coward who left his wife and child at the hands of terrorists.

CHAPTER XXIX

His third trip was to Yosemite National Park. After those three trips Kurt decided to drive to Tucson next over a three-day weekend holiday. The weather was beautiful since it was in the middle of spring. He prepared his Raptor the night before then early in the morning he got on the road with Junior. After an eight-hour drive, they arrived in Tucson. Before driving to the ranch, Kurt took a quick tour in town. There were a lot of changes, and Tucson was growing.

Before sundown Kurt arrived at the ranch. The renters had taken good care of the ranch. Kurt was happy to see the ranch like that. He saw that the renters were working around the barn and said, "Hello, good to see you again. You took great care of the ranch. Thanks. If you don't mind, I'll camp close to the river for the next three days."

They were very happy to see Kurt as well. "Of course. You can camp for as long as you want. If you want, you can stay with us at the house too."

Kurt said, "Thanks."

He picked a camping spot that was far from the ranch house and close to the river. Kurt prepared supper before sundown and he ate with Junior. After sundown, he heard his friends howling. He reflected on his mother, his father, the horses and their livestock. Then the howling came closer to Kurt, and he couldn't ignore them. The animals had come to say hello to him. He told them every detail of what happened after he left to go overseas. The next day he hiked with Junior along the trail he used to hike with his mother and father.

When they got back to the camping site, Kurt saw the neighboring ranch owners were waiting for him. They all hugged, and they invited him to the neighborhood bar. They said, "Don't forget to bring your guitar."

Kurt said, "Okay."

After sundown, he drove to the bar with Junior. When they stepped into the bar, everyone applauded Kurt. They were all shaking his hand said, "Welcome home, hero."

Kurt just smiled, and murmured, "Nowadays nothing stays hidden anymore." He never bragged about what happened in Somalia and Kenya; actually, he was always ashamed. He played his country songs and famous country stars' songs. Everybody was dancing and drinking. They were all nice, polite and hardworking people.

CHAPTER XXX

After teaching and working for two years at the university and hospital, Kurt began to prepare for a two-to-three-week trip overseas. Now he had enough money in his account to afford it. He was planning his first trip to Graz, Austria, to visit Mia's grave and the maxillofacial surgery clinic. He also wanted to visit his mother's home state and relatives, if he could find them in Istanbul. Lastly, he planned to go to Bali, Indonesia, to see the wild animals there. His primary reason for choosing Bali was for the rich exotic animals such as the orangutans, wild monkeys and Sumatran elephants. Kurt wanted to rent a cottage near the forest and find a guide to take him to the different trails to see all those animals.

He arranged a nice hotel in the middle of Taksim, Istanbul. His room came with a daily breakfast, which was an advantage for Kurt. He arranged a hotel in Graz, Austria, in the middle of the famous shopping area. It was an old historic hotel called Schlossberg. Kurt's Graz stop was primarily to visit Mia's grave. At the same time, he was thinking of visiting Mia's parents, Martha, and Bernard, followed by the maxillofacial surgery clinic. He finally bought his flight tickets and arranged for Junior's care when he was gone. There was a doggy daycare close to the university where most of the doctors left their animals when they were out of town, and they were happy with them. His vacation was to begin the first week of June. He prepared one duffle bag for his clothing, and a couple of gifts for his friends.

Kurt woke up very early on his first vacation day. He began the day by dropping off Junior at Carol and Joe's doggy daycare. He then drove back to his house, parked his Ford truck, picked up his duffle bag, and called a rideshare to the airport. He was flying with Turkish Airlines from LA to Istanbul, with a layover in Graz. He bought business class tickets after saving for two years. He was tired, and he could sleep until Istanbul, which was around thirteen hours.

CHAPTER XXXI

After a smooth flight, they reached Istanbul airport "
Turkish airlines was switching plains to Graz at Istanbul
airport", and he switched planes to Graz in Istanbul airport. Two more hours passed, and they reached Graz airport. He took a cab to the Schlossberg hotel, dropped off his bag, then took a long walk through Sparkasse, Houptplatz. He went back to the hotel to shower and sleep. Kurt woke up early the next day. He bought two bunches of red and white roses and went to Mia's grave. He sat down and told her everything, including the details of his move to Los Angeles and his life in California. He always wanted to cry when he was at Mia's grave, but after all the torture he endured, he couldn't cry anymore. He visited the maxillofacial surgery clinic in the afternoon, and everybody was happy to see Kurt again. They asked about Los Angeles and the university. He went with Eskinci to an authentic Austrian restaurant to eat wiener schnitzels and *palachinka* in the evening. Kurt and Eskinci talked about the latest advancements in maxillofacial surgery, and they promised to share their research with each other.

The next morning, Kurt visited Martha and Bernard as he promised. They were waiting for Kurt for breakfast. It was an emotional meeting with them. After an hour of sharing only good memories with them, Kurt left their home to return to the Graz airport to fly to Jakarta, Indonesia, via Istanbul. Between Graz and Istanbul, the flight was shaky. They landed at Istanbul international airport. Kurt had two hours to board the Jakarta flight. He decided to find a restaurant in the airport so he could eat something. He picked a nice Turkish restaurant. He knew some of the Turkish foods by name from his mom. He ate delicious Turkish food, dessert and had a Turkish coffee as well. He arrived at the gate for his flight forty-five minutes before boarding. While he was waiting there, he wrote to Scott to let him know about his whereabouts. He took his business class seat next to the aisle. The seats were very comfortable and business class was right behind first class. While he was waiting on the plane, he texted Carol and Joe to ask about Junior. They sent back a message right away saying that Junior was good and acting normal.

The seat to Kurt's left was empty; business class wasn't full, so it worked out for him. He was able to extend his legs and put his handbag in the empty seat. The Jakarta flight was almost twelve hours, so he decided to read the research papers given to him by Eskinci. Eskinci was a famous surgeon in Europe. While he was reading and enjoying the research papers, the flight attendant asked if he wanted anything to drink or eat. Kurt skipped dinner from the flight attendants because he was still full from the meal at the airport. From time to time he stood up and eventually he decided to sleep for a little bit.

After a four-hour nap, he woke up, washed his face, brushed his teeth and shaved, then went back to his seat. He asked the flight attendant for breakfast, which was a delicious Turkish style meal. His mom had introduced him to Turkish breakfast; she would prepare it for him and his father once a month. Kurt decided to finish the remaining research papers from Eskinci after breakfast. He took a lot of notes on his computer about Eskinci's research. When Kurt needed anything, he would call Eskinci from Los Angeles to get his advice on complicated surgeries. Kurt reviewed his Bali itinerary. He had seven days there, and he didn't want to lose time with unnecessary details.

CHAPTER XXXII

They still had six hours left on the flight to Jakarta when Kurt heard an urgent announcement overhead for a doctor. Kurt waited and thought, "Maybe another doctor on the flight is available." Several minutes passed and a second announcement came in. Kurt waited until the third overhead announcement. Kurt couldn't resist any longer. He pressed the flight attendant button on his armchair, while simultaneously murmuring to himself, "Hopefully nothing serious will ruin my vacation."

The flight attendant came right away, and Kurt introduced himself, "I am Assistant Professor Doctor Kurt West and I work at the Los Angeles Medical School surgery department. Here is my ID. How can I help you?"

The flight attendant desperately answered, "Thank God you are on the flight. We found a young lady in the bathroom bleeding and unconscious. We prepared a seat in the front and laid her down. We transferred the surrounding passengers toward the back, and we isolated her." The flight attendant's name according to her tag was Funda.

Kurt turned to her, "Funda, congratulations, so far you did everything right. I don't know right now what happened, but if I need help, I would like you to have you around."

She looked at Kurt and said, "Of course."

When they approached the front, Kurt saw a beautiful young woman laid on the seat, and two other women, as well as another flight attendant, next to her. Kurt's first impression was that she was having a miscarriage based on his experience at the Kenyan clinic. They saw a lot of patients there and he learned how to care for the obstetric patients from Mia and midwife Shwester Karla. He asked Funda, "Can I talk to the pilot?"

She called the pilot and updated him on the ongoing situation. She said, "He is coming right away."

The pilot was baffled, and asked Kurt, "How can I help you?"

Kurt asked him, "Can we talk a little farther from the other passengers?"

Kurt introduced himself to the pilot, then started to explain the situation, "Captain, you have a passenger right now who might be having a miscarriage. She has had significant blood loss and is unconscious. She needs urgent medical help. My first impression is that she is having an incomplete miscarriage and needs to be immediately transported to a medical facility for an exam and medical intervention."

The pilot said, "We are flying right now at 37,000 feet, and we have 3.5 hours left to our destination. If we can find a proper airport for an emergency landing, it would be in India. It may take at least two hours or more for us to land emergently."

Kurt looked sad and said, "She can't wait that long, and if we wait without doing anything, we may lose her. There may not be much help in your flight medical kit either."

The pilot looked upset and said, "Professor, in this situation I know you will do your best, and I promise I'll do my best."

CHAPTER XXXIII

Kurt turned to Funda and asked her, "Can you please bring me the emergency flight kit?" He was assuming to find some helpful kits in there what he needs.

She answered, "It's already by her seat."

Kurt liked her forethought. He checked the kit. He never expected to find a speculum for a speculum exam, or a vacuum aspiration device. At least they had a saline bag. He thought, "After IV fluids, I can use the same bag for a blood transfusion." Kurt was a universal blood donor; he could transfuse his blood to the patient, but he needed more medications to help her.

He asked the patient's friends her name and they said, "Sevda", then they introduced themselves, "Deniz and Filiz." Kurt asked them, "Is she using any medication right now?"

Filz said, "She was trying to have an abortion with medication, and she probably has the medication with her." They checked her bag and found two different medications. One was Benadryl, and the other one was Misoprostol. After seeing the medication, Kurt murmured to himself, "Thank God." He was right. She was pregnant and taking Misoprostol to have an abortion.

Now it was time to help her. Kurt asked Sevda's friends for privacy then he asked Funda to assist him. Kurt looked at Sevda. She was hemorrhaging. Kurt asked Funda to cover Sevda with a blanket. Funda was ready with the blanket and immediately covered Sevda. Kurt then asked Funda for a blood pressure cuff. He checked Sevda's vital signs including her blood pressure and pulse. Kurt inserted an IV line into Sevda's right arm and gave her a bolus of normal saline for the hemorrhage. After a bag of saline, Kurt checked her vital signs again.

Sevda began to revive herself, but she was still bleeding and passing tissue, so Kurt decided to give her the Misoprostol to help pass the tissue and contract the uterus to stop it from bleeding. He checked her vital signs again. Sevda was still tachycardic and hypotensive but regaining consciousness. He decided to transfuse her with his blood. He gave her more Misoprostol.

Kurt sat down next to her. He transfused his blood into the empty saline bag from his left arm. She was lucky Kurt was a universal blood donor O-. He had had a full checkup before this trip and did not have any infections. Sevda's bleeding started to slow down after fifteen to twenty minutes, but she was still hypotensive and tachycardic. He gave her Benadryl before the blood transfusion. Kurt murmured during the blood transfusion, "God, please help me at this undesirable risky treatment". Taking such a risk all alone in a airplane at thousands feet high, without proper equipment, and without proper medication help a woman losing this much blood was too much for him.By the time the blood transfusion finished, Sevda had stopped bleeding and she was no longer hypotensive or tachycardic. Kurt decided to remove the IV. While he was removing his IV, Sevda opened her eyes, and looked at Kurt quizzically. Kurt said, "Hello beautiful."She smiled and said, "Hello." She was a beautiful woman, but her eyes made her look like a woman who had lost her confidence.

Kurt removed his IV line first then hers. He said, "My name is Kurt West, and I am an assistant professor at the Los Angeles Medical School Surgery Department. I was going on vacation to Bali, Indonesia, and the flight attendants asked for a doctor to help with your emergency. I guess I was the only doctor on the flight. When they found you, you were unconscious, and your vital signs were dangerously abnormal because you had lost a considerable amount of blood. I used every tool we had on the flight, including the medication you had with you, and I transfused my own blood for you. The good news is now you have American cowboy blood." Then Kurt smiled at his own joke. Kurt could read from the beautiful face how she liked his explanation and joke.

She was weak, still laying on the seat. She grabbed Kurt's hand and squeezed it a little bit. She said, "Thank you, cowboy."

Kurt smiled and moved his hand. Funda came over, "We notified Sevda's parents when we found her, and we talked with them again to inform them of Sevda's current condition. They were very happy to hear she is awake again and they send their gratitude to Dr West. They said they are the luckiest mother and father to have their daughter treated by Dr West. The authorities have sent an air ambulance to take Sevda back Istanbul when we land."

Kurt smiled and said, "This is very good news that they are sending an air ambulance. Sevda needs to rest for some time to gain strength again. I guess we still have at least two more hours until we land in Jakarta, and I'll be sitting next to you, beautiful, until we land."

CHAPTER XXXIV

Kurt turned to the Sevda, "Let's play a game until we land to keep both of us busy."

She said, "Okay, I am ready." She was young and gaining strength quickly. Kurt said, "Let's play question and answer. First you ask and I'll answer then I'll ask, and you will answer. Private questions will not be answered."

Sevda said, "My first question is a typical female question. Are you married or living with a girlfriend, or single?"

Kurt answered, "I am not married. I am single."

Kurt asked his question, "What did you study in college, and where do you work?"

Her answer was, "I graduated from the Fine Arts College in Rome, Italy. I have my own business, and I design my own jewelry line. At the same time, I am also a model."

Kurt said, "Wow great! I haven't met a model before."

She smiled and said, "I haven't met a cowboy-professor-doctor before."

Kurt knew she was not only smart but a kind person. She was probably flattering Kurt to show her appreciation to him.

She asked her second question, "Are you a real cowboy, professor?"

Kurt said, "Yes. My parents had a small ranch in Tucson, Arizona, and my father was a horse whisperer. I grew up there and learned how to horse whisper and be a cowboy. This is the only dress code I've known since then." She was pleased by the answer. Kurt asked his question, "Living in a city with such delicious Turkish food, how do you keep your figure?"

She said, "Yes, I love Turkish food, but I excuse myself from lunch and dinner invites. Instead, I work in my workshop."

Kurt liked her answer. She was a hardworking businesswoman and she had work ethics. Kurt was keeping her awake, and it was better under the circumstances.

Then the next question came from her, "Do you have a pet or animal at home?"

Kurt said, "Yes, I have a German shepherd. His name is Junior, and he is staying in a family dog care home right now." The next question came from Kurt, "When you were in Italy, what was your favorite food?"

Her answer was pizza, eggplant parmigiana and tiramisu. She asked, "What is your favorite food, Professor?"

His answer was, "When I was in Graz, Austria, for my residency, I fell in love with Wiener schnitzel, palachinka and Sacher torte. Of course, pizza and tiramisu are favorites as well. I also love menemen and kofte too."

She was excited by Kurt's answers and said, "I love Sacher torte as well. Where did you learn about menemen and kofte?"

Kurt answered, "In a Turkish restaurant."Sevda was relaxed now, and she was much more comfortable. She only had some mild pain. Kurt asked another question, because it was working well, "Do you live with you family or alone?"

She laughed, "This is a private question, but I am going to answer it. I live in a small apartment I bought. I live there alone, but most weekends I go to my parents' house. They have dogs and cats who I love to be with, and they have two horses in a private horse barn."

Kurt said, "Wow, I like that you are an animal lover too."

She asked right away, "Do you still whisper horses?"

Kurt answered, "Yes, I do if I have the time and opportunity. I talk to all kinds of animals if I find a chance to talk to them. I love them. I guess it relieves my anxiety when I talk to them."

Sevda began to admire Kurt more as she talked to him.

Kurt asked her, "You live in the big city so are you a city slicker?"

She said, "Yes. Most of my life has been in the city. I don't know much about outdoor activities." Then she asked Kurt, "Do you play any instruments?"

Kurt said, "Yes, I play the guitar. Before I moved to Graz, I played country music and sang my own songs as well as songs by country stars. In Graz I learned classical guitar music and how to play jazz better."Sevda said, "I don't understand, Dr West. You are every woman's dream man, every woman's desire, every woman would want to live with you. How come you are still single?"

Kurt put a small smile on his face and answered, "Don't forget, we had a small rule, no private questions." Kurt thought about the question. Sevda didn't know how painful her question, was. How he could forget, and forgive himself from all this bad memories. Mia and their unborn child loss, and years long captivity torture by terrorists, and their lingering psychological, and physical effects on him.

Kurt wanted to change the subject, so he asked her another question her, "Do you play a musical instrument, or do you do any outdoor activities?"

She answered, "No I don't play any instruments, and I don't do any outdoor activities, but I go to the gym every day to keep my form. I make a nice living modeling."

Kurt said, "I am sure you do," and smiled.

Sevda didn't waste the opportunity to ask another question right away, "How long will stay in Bali, and what is your plan there?"

Kurt said, "This involves a little bit of privacy, but I am going to answer it. I will stay at Bali for seven days but not in the city. I rented a cottage close to the forest and found a guide to take me every day on different trails to see as many exotic animals as I can. I am not a hunter. I just want to see them as close as I can. I'll fly back to Los Angeles after a four-day stay in Istanbul."

CHAPTER XXXV

They heard the announcement from the pilot. They were going to land in forty-five minutes. Sevda was much better now, and she could even sit up in her seat. Funda came by and explained to them what the arrangements at the airport for Sevda were. She said, "After landing, the airport medical emergency team will come to pick up Sevda with two Turkish Airline agents. They will take her to the airport emergency room to wait for an air ambulance that is coming from Turkey. Sevda's friends and I will accompany her. As far as I know, Sevda's mom will be arriving with the air ambulance to accompany her daughter back to Turkey."

Kurt liked what he heard. It was good news for Sevda.

He said, "After we land, you will be in good hands, and this nightmare will end."

She looked at Kurt's face and said, "It's just the opposite. I was in safe hands on this airplane. I can't imagine anybody else would have saved my life like you did." Tears started to come down her beautiful face.

Kurt didn't want to get emotional and said, "You are a very strong and beautiful woman. You will overcome this quickly and forget this happened to you."

Kurt stood up from his seat, "The time has come for me to go back to my seat and get ready for the landing."

Sevda was still holding onto Kurt's hand and said, "Please come back and stay with me until the plane lands."

Kurt answered, "I checked your vital signs several minutes ago, and you are doing well. You don't need me anymore. I will ask your friends to come over and stay with you."

She said, "Please," again.

Kurt smiled and decided to stay with her. He also enjoyed talking to someone who was so fun and beautiful. He said, "Okay, I'll be back in a couple minutes after I grab my bag." She let go of his hand. Before getting his bag, Kurt stopped by Sevda's friends and explained her condition to them. He stopped at the restroom and washed his face with cold water. He picked up his bag and went back to Sevda. The minute she saw Kurt again she smiled. She grabbed Kurt's hand again.

Now it was time for Kurt to tell her about her treatment. He told her shortly what he had done, and he explained to her, "I will write a detailed report when I am on the Bali flight, and I'll email it to you as soon as the airplane lands. I will not send this report to anybody else unless I must. I heard from your friends that your parents are both medical doctors. If you allow me to, I can share the report with them so they can decide your future treatment, if necessary. Right now, you don't need any more treatment other than an ultrasound. All you need is rest and rehabilitation. You are strong now that you have cowboy blood in your veins, but there is a small problem with this; you might become a cowgirl and lose your modeling job, Beautiful."

She laughed for the first time since Kurt saw her. After a while she asked again, "Where will you stay in Istanbul?"

Kurt answered, "Remember we had a rule, no private questions, but I'll answer it. I'll stay in Taksim at the Divan Hotel, which has a high rating."

She said, "Good choice, Kurt." She was calling him by his first name now. They heard an announcement for landing while they were talking. Funda asked if they needed anything as they made their final descent. Sevda looked into Kurt's eyes and said, "I wish you could stay with me longer. You are a very good doctor, a very handsome cowboy and a brave man, Kurt. Don't forget, I am a woman just like all the other women who would love to be with you. I know I am in a vulnerable situation right now, but I'll be waiting for you in Istanbul to show you the real Sevda."

Kurt responded to her, "You are a beautiful, kind, skillful, entertaining, vulnerable and strong woman. Every man in the world wants a woman like you. I am sure you have unlimited admirers in Istanbul. As for me, I am a lonely cowboy and doctor. I was coincidently on this airplane, and I did my job like any other doctor would. You impressed me because you were vulnerable and now you are getting stronger. You will forget me after I am gone."

Those were the last words they said to one another before Kurt walked off the airplane. She was still holding Kurt's hand. Kurt kissed her from cheek to cheek and walked out. Sevda's friends approached her, and Kurt said goodbye to them both. At the airplane exit a surprise was waiting for Kurt. All the flight attendants and pilots were waiting in a line. The minute they saw Kurt, they started to applaud.

Funda said, "Dr West I would fly anywhere with you if you wanted me."

Then the pilot shook Kurt's hand and said, "Thank you, Dr West, we will always remember you." It was a very good gesture from the flight crew.

Kurt said, "I thank you all," and walked out the door.

CHAPTER XXXVI

After passport control, Kurt passed the airport's domestic flight section and found his Bali flight gate. He had two hours, so he sat down to write a text message to Scott. He sent another text message to the dog care guys, Carol and Joe, to ask about Junior. He took out his computer from his bag and wrote a detailed report about Sevda's treatment. While he was writing the report, he was thinking about her. Kurt was affected by her a lot, but he wasn't ready for another relationship yet. He couldn't stop thinking about how the terrorists killed Mia with their child. Kurt was just beginning to get himself together again, and if he had another failed relationship that ended with loss, he knew it would be the end of him.

It was time for Kurt to move on. He had saved money and vacation time for this trip so he could enjoy the exotic animals and environment. Kurt focused on finishing Sevda's report so he could email it to her. He detailed every step he used to treat her and finished the report on the Jakarta–Bali flight. He emailed her after they landed in Bali.

Kurt saw a guy holding a sign with his name on it at the airport exit. Kurt thought, "He should be the local guide," and walked up to him.

He had a smile on his face, and introduced himself, "I am Nyoman, your guide, but you can call me Ahmad."

Kurt shook Ahmad's hand, and said, "I am Kurt."

Ahmad said, "Follow me, Kurt. I parked my truck in the parking lot. We will drive to your cottage today. If you want to go grocery shopping, let's do that before leaving town."

Kurt said, "Okay, let's stop at the food market." They stopped at a big food market and Kurt shopped for food for himself after asking Ahmad what food he needed for the trip. They reached the cottage that evening. The cottage was a one-bedroom, one-bathroom space. It was okay for Kurt because he would be outdoors most of the time.

Ahmad carried Kurt's bags inside and said, "I'll be back tomorrow very early in the morning. My village is just north of here, about ten minutes. Tomorrow I'll bring all the hiking and camping gear. The plan for tomorrow is to hike Mount Agung, which takes twelve hours one way."

Then Ahmad left Kurt at the cottage alone. Kurt decided to go to sleep early, and he ate a snack before going to bed. Before falling asleep, he began to dream of Mia. He was very comfortable and happy with her, and an unfortunate, and dreadful terrorist raid took her and their child away. As Kurt was dreaming of Mia, another beautiful pretty face and smile began to take the place of Mia's image was looking

like Sevda. This was a surprise for Kurt, and it was scary because a dream like this hadn't happened to him before. She was grabbing Kurt's hand and smiling at him. Her eyes were shining, and she was asking him not to go.

CHAPTER XXXVII

Ahmad arrived at four o'clock in the morning with a cup of coffee and baked goods from his wife. Kurt enjoyed the coffee and pastries. They drove to Mont Agung. Ahmad parked his truck and unloaded the equipment. They split the equipment into two loads and placed them in large, fortified backpacks. There was nobody around this early in the morning. They started the challenging twelve-hour hike. Kurt was guessing how many times Ahmad did this hike for a living, and assumed it was probably more than twenty times. Ahmad was carrying a rifle with him just in case they encountered a Sumatran tiger. According to Ahmad, they did not hang around Mont Agung.

The first hour of walking in the dark was easy. When the sun started to rise, they took their first break. The backpacks added extra weight and made the hike more difficult. They resumed walking after a ten-minute rest. Ahmad couldn't believe Kurt's pace. Most of his customers slowed down dramatically after the first stop, but Kurt was even better than himself. They were walking at a steady pace now while Kurt looked at the surrounding environment in wonder.

The trail was surrounded by dense foliage. The birds were smelling the flowers and singing. The surrounding nature was beautiful to Kurt. He was coming from a big city, and previously had only spent time in the desert. After nearly five hours had passed, they decided to take a thirty-minute break to eat a snack and rest. After eating, Kurt looked around to see if he could find some animals, and asked Ahmad for advice. Ahmad smiled and said, "I am sure you can hear the monkeys; they are all around, but they haven't come out yet. They will come if we stay a little longer in the same area. They are mostly friendly unless you get close and try to touch them, and then they bite."

Kurt smiled and started to get ready to hike again. Now they were almost halfway up the summit, but they were getting tired and the next six hours would be hard for them. The weather began to get warmer and more humid, which slowed them down dramatically. They drank more liquid to avoid dehydration and muscle cramps.

Around six hours later, and after a couple more stops, they reached the top of the summit. Kurt couldn't believe his eyes at how beautiful the view was from the top. You couldn't dream of such beauty without seeing it. They identified their camp area before sunset and prepared their tents for the night. Ahmad was like Kurt, he didn't talk much unless Kurt asked him questions, but he was an avid outdoorsman. Kurt had been lucky to find him. Ahmad knew the environment very well and he had brought whatever they might need for the trip.

When night fell, Kurt lay down in his sleeping bag outside of the tent. He counted the stars in the sky and called them by the names he had given them when he was in captivity in Somalia. The sky was beautiful here like the Somalian desert sky. His wish had been to escape from captivity at the hands of the terrorists and see Mia and their child whenever he saw a falling star, but now he had no dreams and wishes. He was looking at the sky now to refresh his memories, and to remember both the good and bad days. He eventually fell asleep.

The next day Kurt woke up to the smell of coffee. Abdul brought Kurt a cup of coffee, and they began to prepare for their descent. Kurt and Abdul began their hike down the trail very early in the morning. Walking downhill with the heavy backpacks was much easier, and this gave Kurt more time and focus to look at his surrounding environment and animals.

After a couple of hours, Kurt saw that the monkeys were watching them and following them. He pointed them out to Ahmad, who said, "They will try to come close to us, but don't worry, they won't harm us."

Kurt said, "I don't worry, I just want to spend some time with them."

Ahmad said, "Okay, we will stop when they come close to us." They took off their backpacks and ate a snack with some water. While they were eating, the monkeys started to make some movement toward them.

Kurt turned to Ahmad said, "I'll talk with them for a while, and if you want you can take a nap."

Ahmad looked at Kurt strangely and said, "Okay." After Ahmad lay down for a nap far from Kurt, he started to tell the monkeys what happened on his way to the Jakarta flight. The monkeys fell silent and looked at Kurt as the good listeners that they were. Once Kurt finished talking, he said to them, "Thank you very much for listening to me." He woke Ahmad up so they could resume hiking again. They finished hiking before sundown, and Ahmad left Kurt at his cottage. Kurt didn't waste any time taking a shower and immediately jumped into bed.

The next morning, Ahmad arrived again around 4:30 a.m. with coffee and pastries. Kurt got ready right away and said, "Thanks for the coffee and for your wife's delicious pastries." They drove to the West Bali National Park for hiking. Kurt was expecting to see more wild animals on this hike. They parked the truck at the base of the trail and began their hike at the very well preserved national forest. The hike would take at least eight hours. The foliage was very dense, and the color was so beautiful. After walking for a couple of hours, they saw a muntjac (barking deer) herd. They sounded horrible and Kurt began to laugh at them. After watching the herd, they recommenced hiking. Wild pigs began to surround them, along with monkeys.

After taking a lunch break, they finished the hike. They finished the hike early in the afternoon so they could get more time to rest for the next day's hike. Ahmad dropped Kurt off at his cottage. After a long shower, Kurt sat down on the porch and listened to the sounds coming from deep inside the forest. There wasn't any cell phone or internet service, so he had some time to rest his mind. He slowly went back to bed again.

The beautiful smell of coffee and pastry woke Kurt up again early in the morning. Their hike today would be the Mount Batur volcano summit. Kurt was not expecting to see animals on this hike, but he was looking forward to seeing the temple at the top of the mountain. After a seven-hour hike, they reached the summit and the small temple. From the top view was gorgeous. You could also see the beautiful Lake Braton from top of the mountain. They spent some time at this location and took some pictures, then hiked back home.

The following day's hike was a little bit more challenging. It was the Munduk jungle hike. They started their day with coffee and pastries again. Kurt turned to Ahmad, and said, "You know what I'll miss most when I go back to Los Angeles? I will miss your wife's coffee and pastries every morning."

Ahmad laughed, and said, "She will love this when she hears it."

They started their hike early again. They picked the challenging Dutch Colonial trail. Kurt was hoping to see orangutans and Sumatran tigers. In the middle of the hike, Kurt saw that a young tiger was looking at them from the branch of a tree. Kurt warned Ahmad and said, "Ahmad don't aim your rifle at her. Instead stand still and let me handle this. If you see her charging at us, then you can shoot her." Kurt stood still where he was and looked directly into the tiger's eyes. Kurt's and the tiger's eyes locked. Kurt said to her, "Look, we will neither harm you nor stay here. We are just on a hike and enjoying the beautiful jungle. We know this is your territory and we will obey your rules." The tiger kept her eyes on Kurt while she jumped down from the tree and ran deep into the jungle. Kurt looked at the tiger as she left, and he was shaking.

Abdul came up to Kurt and said, "I can't believe this. You talked to the tiger, then she ran into the jungle."

Kurt said, "I can't believe it too." They recommenced their hike. Kurt said to himself, "Hopefully we won't see another tiger again."

They heard the orangutans shriek from inside the jungle, but they didn't encounter them. After Abdul dropped Kurt off at his cottage, Kurt took a long shower, and sat down on the chair on the porch. He was still shaking. It had been a dangerous encounter with a wild beast, but either they were lucky, or the animal figured they were friendly hikers.

The last two days they hiked Sangeh, and Uluwatu Monkey Forest. On both hikes, Kurt found a lot of opportunities to get close to the monkeys and talk to them. Kurt enjoyed their friendship a lot and told them what happened when they encountered the tiger. It was time to say farewell to Bali and Ahmad. Kurt gave Amhad and his wife a nice tip. Ahmad was still smiling while he drove Kurt to the airport, probably because he didn't expect a tip like that, but he and his wife deserved it.

Before Kurt get of the truck at the airport Ahmad said, "Mister West I will hike anywhere in the world with you. You have a sacred relationship with animals. They all listen to you. I believe this is a gift from God to you. I wish you safe travels."

Kurt smiled, shook his hand and said goodbye.

CHAPTER XXXVIII

Kurt had some time to get on the plane. When he sat down, he checked his phone for the first time since arriving in Bali. There were a lot of emails and text messages. He could not read and answer all of them. He first read Scott's message checking on him, asking if everything was okay and letting him know he was waiting on Kurt's return. Kurt answered him with a short message, "Everything is going well. I'll be flying to Istanbul soon. I missed you too." He read Carol and Joe's message second. They gave an update on Junior. He was good and enjoying playtime with the other dogs. Kurt liked this good news. He went to his third message, which was from Beautiful, "Dear Kurt, I know you do not have an internet or phone connection where you are. I wanted to thank you for your detailed medical report. I gave it to my parents to read. They both admired your knowledge, courage and sacrifice. Every moment, every minute, every hour, and every day I remember what happened to me, and I consider myself lucky, because you were on the same flight as me. I am staying right now with my parents and getting stronger every day. I am holding my breath until I see you again in Istanbul. Please, if you find an opportunity, let me know about your departure to Istanbul. With love, Sevda."

Kurt smiled and thought about what an emotional and open-hearted woman she was. She expressed her feelings, regardless of what Kurt thought about her. This was a unique quality, and this vulnerable quality made her even more beautiful and more desirable. Kurt didn't know what was happening to him. He couldn't dream about just Mia anymore because Sevda would intrude into his dream, and this was scaring Kurt. Kurt decided to send a text message to her, "Dear Sevda, thank you very much for contacting me. After a wonderful, entertaining, educating and extraordinarily fascinating visit to the Bali wilderness, I feel tired. I am sure I'll regain my energy on the way to Istanbul while on the flight to see one of the most beautiful, exciting, mystical cities, and you. I'll call you as soon as I can."

The flight was on time. Kurt read all his emails on the flight to Jakarta. He was tired and fell asleep on the flight. He checked into the Istanbul flight. He had a business class seat, which was comfortable, and he had a better chance to rest until Istanbul. While he was trying to sleep, the flight attendant came by, and asked if he wanted anything. Kurt recognized the chief flight attendant Funda.

She smiled and said, "Dr West, the flight crew and I am very happy to see you on our flight."

Kurt smiled and said, "I am very happy to fly with you again."

CHAPTER XXXIX

Kurt woke up as the airplane was landing at Istanbul airport, and the view from the airplane was magnificent. After walking out of the airport, he took a taxicab to the Divan Hotel. It was afternoon, and the traffic was very heavy. The hotel was new. They gave him a room partially with a view of the Bosporus and partially view the city. On the nightstand was a beautiful bouquet of flowers in a bucket, a box of chocolates and an envelope. He opened the envelope which said, "Hello Kurt, I am enjoying my coffee down in the lobby. After your shower, come join me and I'll show you Istanbul, Sevda."

Kurt took a long and relaxing shower, then he took a clean pair of jeans and shirt from his bag, put on his boots and walked down to the lobby. He saw Sevda, who was looking at her cell phone. She looked healthy, confident and more appealing. She was dressed colorfully and had some light summer makeup on.

When she saw Kurt, she stood up and hugged him, saying, "Welcome to Istanbul, my hero cowboy."

Kurt looked at her, smiled and said, "I am very happy to see you again, Beautiful. Thank you very much for the flowers and chocolates. You spoil me a lot. In fact, I am not used to being spoiled like this."

She said, "It's evening now, let's go have dinner and talk. I think I'll be the first Turkish woman around to go to dinner with a cowboy. Please just smile when someone takes our picture when we are together. You are already famous. Everybody knows how you saved my life on the Jakarta flight."

Kurt was surprised again. She took him to a beautiful fish restaurant in the Bosporus. When they got to the restaurant, everybody turned around and stared at them. She was a famous model, and Kurt was a cowboy accompanying her. They sat down at their reserved table. Sevda ordered a glass of white wine for herself and a beer for Kurt. Kurt became aware of this and said, "I am not a drinker. If I drink, I only drink one kind of beer."

She smiled, "Don't worry, just feel comfortable."

CHAPTER XXXX

After a couple of sips from her wine, Sevda began to talk, "I just want to explain to you why I was having miscarriage."

Kurt cut her off right away, "Look, Beautiful, you don't have to explain anything to me. It just happened between you and your boyfriend. Now it's gone and you are healthy again."

She said, "No, I want to explain. I don't have a boyfriend right now. I broke up with him two months ago. He was a rich and prominent family's son. I was like the other women in town chasing guys like him, although my family was against it. He was cheating on me. I think his thought was, I am rich, I can do whatever I want. When I told him I was pregnant, he became nervous. He told his family, and his family became angry with me, because they are conservative when it comes to pregnancy. They didn't like the idea of being pregnant before marriage, so I decided to break up with him. Honestly, he didn't care much that I broke up with him. For him, his family's wealth was much more important than the pregnancy and mine. I didn't want a baby from a guy I didn't love anymore. I talked with my doctor, and she gave me those pills. My friends and I saw you on the flight. We also had a Bali vacation plan. I started the pills then I paused them irresponsibly. You know what happened to me next. I am very sorry, Kurt. Fortunately, the three or four hours being with you on the airplane changed my entire life. You are the most talented doctor. You are brave, and the most handsome cowboy in this world."

Kurt listened to her with a smile on his face and without interrupting.

She took another sip of her wine and resumed speaking, "When you came close to me on the airplane, before treating me, you were murmuring to yourself. I was still conscious, and I heard your secret unintentionally. I also read everything about you on Google. You are a real hero, Kurt. You sacrificed yourself for your family and friends. Terrorists tortured you for almost three years. You lost your wife and child, and without any hesitation you sacrificed yourself for me, a person you don't know and a woman you may never see again. You are a real hero, and I love you." Her eyes started to water and tear drops fell down her face.

She continued to talk, "I love you, and I am lucky to know a person like you. I love you because I am very lucky to get close to you. Millions of women wouldn't have a chance to know a person like you and fall in love. After you, my life started to change fast. I don't go out to clubs or bars anymore. I don't hang around my old hangouts. I work at my workshop for more hours, and my family has become friendlier with me again." She was looking at Kurt's eyes with wet eyes.

Kurt said, "So you know how terrorists killed my wife?"

She said, "I am sorry, I didn't want to hide this from you after everything you did for me."

Kurt said, "Thanks, you did the right thing. Not many people know what happened to my family. I quietly hid this from everybody like coworkers in university. People who they were at the clinic where the incident happened, they never talks about Mia's loss with me, because they know I still hold my self-responsible for Mia's and our child's loss."

She said, "You tried to save them like you tried to save me. If I had died, it wouldn't have been your fault. You are not a coward, you take risks when you must, and I feel safe around you. I know you would protect me again."

Kurt didn't know what to say. It was a pivotal point, and he was a lonely cowboy who didn't know how to respond. He waited a couple of minutes, then said, "You know what I like about you so much? You are an honest woman. Your inside is the same as your outside. They are both beautiful and you hold no secrets. You express your feelings without hesitation. Millions of people, including me, don't know how to express their feelings, or we don't even know our feelings, unlike you. You have a gift, please don't lose it."

She stood up and came close to Kurt and kissed him on the cheek. Although everybody in the restaurant was looking at them, Kurt loved her excitement. After finishing their dinner, Sevda asked for the bill, but Kurt didn't let her pay. As they were leaving the restaurant Sevda grabbed Kurt's hand as they walked out. Outside by the door several press members and paparazzi were waiting for them. The minute they stepped outside the restaurant, paparazzies, press, and tv speakers all surrounded Sevda and Kurt. Questions were coming from all directions, and cameras were recording them and taking pictures from every angle. Kurt didn't understand any of the questions, and just smiled like Sevda told him to. Sevda talked to the media for several minutes. She was very good at handling them. She then grabbed Kurt's hand and they walked to Sevda's car.

She said, "Everybody around the world knows you are a hero and an excellent doctor. From now on, you are a celebrity in Turkey."

Kurt laughed a lot at this. He said, "Wow, I became celebrity". Kurt smiled "at least for now I enjoy being a celebrity and I like how you handled the press."

She smiled and said, "Thank you for flattering me, it's very good to hear from you." She drove them to a famous café on top of the hills with a beautiful view of Istanbul. They both ordered Turkish coffee and Sevda said, "Tomorrow I planned a visit to the historical sites, and it will take all day, if that's okay with you."

Kurt said, "That's fine for me. I was planning the same thing, but you don't have to accompany me."

She smiled "Are you kidding me? Don't you see how happy I am with you? I am grateful I have a chance to be with a person like you. I am praying every minute, every hour, every day, and I thank God gave me a chance like this."

Kurt looked into her eyes and said, "I don't think I deserve that much flattery. I told you before I did what I did do like every other doctor does every day."

She said, "No, Kurt, you are a very modest and decent person. You are punishing yourself because of the unexpected and unfortunate things that happened to you. You don't value yourself for all the good things you have done."

Kurt wanted to change the subject, so he asked Sevda, "What time did you plan our historic tour for tomorrow?"

She said, "I'll be at the hotel around seven o'clock, then we'll go to a place where they are just serving breakfast." Kurt said, "Okay, but I want to eat menemen, sucuk, pastirma and puacha."

She asked, "How do you know all these special breakfast foods?"

Kurt smiled, "You see Google doesn't know everything. My mom, Ece, was a Turkish woman."

The minute Sevda heard this, she leapt from her seat and kissed Kurt on his cheek then said loudly, "God, I can't believe this! The more I know about you, the more I fall in love with you. Tell me are you real and that all these things are really happening!" She was standing by Kurt with her hands on her cheeks in astonishment.

Kurt softly grabbed her hand and seated her in the chair and started to talk, "Ece had a tourist gift store in Anadolu, Hisari, and my dad was in service at a base in Turkey. One day my father traveled to Istanbul to take a tourist boat to see Bosporus. The boat stopped at Istanbul for a couple of hours, and my father wanted to buy some gifts for a friend. He saw my mom's shop. They met for the first time. Over time, my father convinced my mother to marry him. After my father's service was over, they moved to Tucson, Arizona, and lived at my father's small ranch."

Sevda listened to the entire story with her open mouth, flabbergasted.

Kurt said, "This is why I stopped in Istanbul. After tomorrow, I'll go Anadolu Hisari to see if her store is still there, and to see if I can find any relatives of hers."

She looked into Kurt's eyes, "No, Kurt, we will go together and look if we can find someone who still knows your mom. I am not going to leave you alone in Istanbul. I am sure every woman wants to have you and now that you are a celebrity let's see what will come out about you from the press tomorrow."

CHAPTER XXXXI

Kurt was ready and waiting for Sevda at 7:00 a.m. in the lobby. She walked in in a hurry and a big smile on her face. She was very stylishly dressed and had on a moderate amount of makeup. She had brought several papers and magazines with her. She showed them to Kurt. All of them had Sevda's and Kurt's pictures from yesterday as they exited the restaurant. They were both smiling, hand in hand. She said, "I don't like to say this, but I told you so. They say that Sevda is in love with the cowboy professor. They are not lying. They are right about that." She looked deep into Kurt's eyes.

Kurt smiled and said, "Let's go have breakfast." They both ate a delicious Turkish breakfast while a lot of smiling eyes were on them. Sevda rushed Kurt from one historical site to another. They were all well protected and preserved. She always kept Kurt's hand in hers. Kurt didn't complain about it. He wasn't a person who expressed his feelings easily, and he didn't know how. Hanging around Sevda made him happy. On the way to dinner at an authentic old Istanbul restaurant, Sevda showed Kurt her apartment as they passed by.

It appeared to be in a nice neighborhood. Dinner was very good, and they talked about everything they liked and disliked. Kurt said to Sevda, "The press isn't following us today, I guess we are lucky."

Sevda smiled, "They respect you and they love you. In Turkey, everybody loves heroes, wherever they are or wherever they come from. Besides, you saved my life by transfusing your own blood and putting yourself in danger. You will always be a celebrity in Turkey. If they hear that your mom is Turkish, they will line up for a chance to interview you."

CHAPTER XXXXII

The next morning Sevda arrived at 7:00 a.m. again and they ate breakfast at the hotel. It was excellent. After breakfast they rushed to catch the tourist boat. They sat outside while on the boat and it was breezy. Sevda was holding Kurt's hand, enjoying the beautiful view and smell of the ocean sea.

Kurt was thinking, "Probably this was the same kind of boat my father traveled on to Anadolu Hisari." Around lunchtime, they arrived at Anadolu Hisari. Kurt was excited to see his mother's relatives and to see if the gift shop was still there. They walked down the main street looking for a gift shop, and they saw several of them, but they were all new buildings. Kurt didn't know his mother's Turkish last name. He became sad and hopeless. They asked all the gift shop attendants if they knew someone by the name of Ece. All their answers were negative. The gift shop owners were young, and they were not originally from Anadolu Hisari.

Sevda could read Kurt's face very well. She put her head on his shoulder, "I feel what you are feeling right now. We could find a clue from the mayor's office, but they are closed for the holiday. If we could find your mom's Turkish last name, we could look up her relatives. I will come back next week to talk to the town census clerk. Maybe I can find her Turkish last name and relatives."

Kurt said, "You don't have to, but thanks anyway."

They both were so sad; they couldn't eat their lunch. They got on the boat again. The boat crossed to the Bosporus European side. Sevda told Kurt, "We will get off the boat here. I want to show you my workshop because it's close to here." They took a taxicab and ten minutes later they were standing in front of a historical building. She said, "My workshop is in this building. The building belongs to my parents, but I still pay them rent for this, although I pay a discounted rate because they are not happy to get my money."

Kurt liked the building; it was very well preserved. They walked into the studio. Two young designers were working when they arrived. The studio was decorated with design artwork. It was plain and very well illuminated. The two young designers approached Kurt and introduced themselves.

Sevda showed her work to Kurt, all of which was designed by her. They were all beautiful works of art, and they reflected Sevda's elegance, beauty, kindness and pure heart.

Kurt came close to Sevda and kissed her on the cheek. He said, "They are all beautiful like you, congratulations."

Sevda was baffled and looked at Kurt speechless. She said, "You can kiss me if you want from my lips as well."

Kurt didn't resist her, he was thinking that if this would make her happy, he'd do it, so he kissed her softly on the lips.

She put her arms around Kurt's neck and started to yell, "Oh my God! Oh my God! You kissed me, you kissed me. I am the happiest woman in world right now!" The other designers looked at them with a smile. Before they left Sevda's workshop, Sevda took her thin summer scarf from her neck and tied it around Kurt's left elbow. She said while looking at Kurt adoringly, "Kurt, please keep this with you as a good luck charm. I designed this for you. If you miss me, just look at the scarf or you can smell me."

They took another taxicab to Sevda's car which was parked at the pier. While Sevda was driving, she said, "If you mind, we don't have to go there, but my parents have a small party for you. I understand if you don't like this kind of social gathering. We can go to a belly dancer restaurant instead so we can have some fun."

Kurt looked at her face said, "I wouldn't mind getting together with your parents and friends."

She grabbed his hand again and said, "Thank you very much, Kurt. You are a very kind person. They all know your mom was a Turkish woman. If they ask anything about your past or activities, you don't have to answer them. Enjoy the special food and music. My parents arranged a small orchestra."

CHAPTER XXXXIII

Her parents lived on the Bosporus hillside in a beautiful two-story villa. They had a pool, a well-cared-for back and front yard, two Chinese pugs and two Bulldogs. The dogs greeted Sevda and Kurt before everybody else. Kurt talked to them and treated them like every other animal. The dogs wagged their tails in return and followed Kurt around for the remainder of the day. Sevda looked at the dogs and smiled. They walked into the saloon which was nearly full with twenty guests. Two of them came to the front of the crowd. Sevda introduced them as her father and mother.

They were a nice-looking couple. Her father said right away, "It's an honor to meet with you Dr West. We were very lucky that you were serendipitously on the same flight as Sevda. If my wife or I would have been there, we couldn't treat her like you treat. We will never forget your skillful treatment our daughter. Please enjoy the party. Most of the folks here are doctors and they wanted to see a brave doctor like you."

Sevda's mother replied, "Dr West, thank you very much, but these two words will never express our gratitude to you. You didn't conquer only my family's heart but everybody who hears about your sacrifice and courage."

Kurt smiled at them both, "Thank you very much for your kind words and for flattering me. I am sure under the same circumstances every other doctor, including you, would have found a way to save this beautiful woman."

They both walked to the buffet, which looked incredibly good. Sevda took two plates, "I will fill your plate as well, and so far, I know what you enjoy."

Kurt smiled, "Okay." He grabbed a beer for himself and a glass of Chablis for Sevda. Every guest in the room was coming up to Sevda and Kurt and praising him with kind words. Beautiful night music came from the poolside. The band consisted of one young woman and a three-musician orchestra.

Sevda picked a location where there weren't a lot of guests and said, "Let's enjoy the food and drink a while without interruption."

Kurt enjoyed the delicious food and said, "Thanks, Beautiful, you picked the right stuff."

She smiled, "Thank you very much for your dance invitation," and grabbed Kurt's hand. They started to dance where they were. She said, "You are a good dancer, Kurt."

He smiled, "You have to see my Western dance," then laughed at his own joke. He continued, "When we were kids, the girls hated my Western dance. They said I was having more fun than them."

Sevda said, "One day I am sure you will teach me Western dance."

Kurt said, "It would be a pleasure to teach dance to a beautiful woman like you."

She kissed Kurt's cheek, "Can I ask you a favor? I know you are a very good musician. Will you play us some?"

Kurt said, "I am a musician. I don't know if I am a good musician, but I'll play for you."

She grabbed Kurt's hand, and they walked through the party to the orchestra. Sevda took a guitar case and gave it to Kurt, "This is a gift from me. I engraved an image of myself on the backside of the guitar. That means you'll be the last owner."

Kurt couldn't believe his eyes. It was a vintage original Martin D-45. Its value was probably around $10,000. He turned the guitar over and there was a woman that looked like Sevda engraved into the wood with a cowboy on a horse that looked like Kurt. There was an inscription that said, "From Sevda, with love." Kurt kissed her on the cheek, "Thanks, Beautiful, but I can't accept this very expensive gift from you, but I can play tonight with. This is a Martin D-45 original vintage guitar. I've never played one like this before. I am sure it will be pleasure."

Kurt took the guitar and spoke with the young musicians a little bit then sat down on a chair. He started to play Europe's very well-known Manitas De Plata's "Capes Et Piques" followed by "Nature Boy" by Eden Abez. Finally, he played two of his own country songs. Sevda was looking into his eyes warmly and affectionately. Kurt thanked the musicians and then came by Sevda. Her eyes were full of tears and admiration. There was a shout of "Bravo!" from the guests.

Kurt turned to Sevda and said, "I think it's time for me to go back to the hotel. I don't want you to drop me off at the hotel. I can take a taxicab."

She said, "You know I am not going to let you do that, and on the way to the hotel I'll tell you about tomorrow's plan, which is our last day together."

On the way back to the hotel she said, "Surprise! Tomorrow we will do something you love. We will ride horseback along the Black

Sea coast. Before riding, if you want, you can try the horses at the stall, and you can give me instructions on how to accompany you."

Kurt turned to Sevda, "Of course, I love it."

Before Kurt got out of the car, Sevda approached him and said, "You forgot something before you left," and showed her lips to Kurt.

Kurt turned and kissed her softly and said, "See you tomorrow morning."

CHAPTER XXXIV

Early in the morning, Sevda's phone rang. She barely read the time on the phone, it was 4.30 a.m., and the caller ID showed Kurt's name and number. She answered right away, "Good morning, cowboy."

Kurt said, "I am waiting for you in front of your apartment. It's better to go horseback riding early." She jumped out of bed and ran to the window to look down into the street. There was a cowboy down there leaning against Sevda's car. Kurt had his hat on him.

She said, "If you want, you can come up here, otherwise I'll be down there in ten minutes." She came down ten minutes later and said, "Wow, there is a real cowboy waiting for me in Istanbul."

Kurt had two coffees and a package with him. He said, "I see you in jeans and boots for the first time. You look like a Western girl."

She jumped into Kurt's arms and kissed him on the cheek, "By the way, how did you come here?"

Kurt replied, "If you remember, you showed me your apartment before and I remembered the street name and the building number, so the taxicab driver found it easily. I brought coffee and pastries from the hotel. They were looking delicious."

They got into the car and drove to Sevda's family's horse stable. The place was surrounded with trees and a green pasture. They parked the car and walked into the office. There was a café next to the office so before they walked to see the horses, they drank their coffees and ate their pastries.

Sevda grabbed Kurt's hand, "Let's go to see Ruzgar and Tezcan. Ruzgar is my horse and Tezcan is my father's."

The stall was very clean, and two workers were feeding and cleaning the horses. Sevda showed their horses to Kurt. Kurt liked them; they were well taken care of. Kurt said, "Okay, can you sit and wait one hour so I can the prepare horses?"

She said, "I'll be waiting at the café. Please don't spend a lot of time with the horses because this will make me jealous."

Kurt smiled and went to the horses. Almost one hour later he walked out of the stall with the two horses walking behind him and sat by Sevda. She was excited and said, "How come they follow you so quietly and calmly? Usually, they are rebelling against us."

Kurt said, "That's the cowboy magic."

While Sevda had been waiting, she asked the café to prepare them sandwiches and drinks for their ride. Kurt helped Sevda mount Ruzgar. Then they rode to the black seacoast. Kurt showed some easy ways to command the horse, although Sevda was already a good rider.

All day long they rode from one shore to another. They would get off the horses and walk hand in hand on the sand. Sevda was unusually quiet. She was looking into Kurt's eyes most of the time and listening to him. If Kurt asked a question, she would answer him. Before sundown they came back to the stall to return the horses. Sevda finally said, "I guess we are both hungry. Let's go back to the city to find a place for dinner."

Sevda drove to a casual restaurant. They picked a quiet table far from curious eyes. Sevda was looking sad, and she appeared as if she was ready to cry. Kurt was aware of it and was talking about his Bali hike to divert her attention. Sevda said, "I guess we must drive back to the hotel. You probably need to get ready for your flight."

Kurt said, "I guess we should. It will not be easy to go back after all the surprises and beautiful things that happened. This vacation was the best thing that has happened to me after all the tragedies. There is no easy way to thank you for your hospitality."

Sevda said, "You don't have to say anything." They drove back to the hotel and got out of the car. Kurt walked beside her, and she was crying. She said, "I don't want to say goodbye to someone I love."

Kurt said, "Don't say goodbye." He showed her the scarf on his elbow, "You will be always with me. As you said, if I miss you, I will smell the scarf."

She said, "You will always be with me. I have your blood in my veins." She kissed Kurt for a long time, then got in her car and drove away.

Kurt left the hotel early the next morning after a good breakfast. He took a taxicab to the Istanbul airport, and after passing through passport control, he boarded the Los Angeles flight. His ticket was business class, but someone was sitting in his seat. Kurt called the flight attendant to ask if this was a mistake. She smiled at Kurt and said, "Please follow me, Dr West. Your seat was upgraded by our company to first class. You are on our honor list." She showed him a front row seat in first class. She was still smiling, "Please let me know if you need anything, it's a pleasure to serve you."

Kurt was of course very happy to travel in first class.

He decided to re-evaluate his feelings for Sevda. It appeared that Sevda was in love with Kurt, and she was expressing her love at every opportunity. She was a woman who didn't hide her feelings to anybody. Her inside and outside were the same. She expressed her feelings very easily. As for Kurt, it was totally the opposite. Expressing his feelings had been very difficult for him before he met Mia, and after Mia it became almost impossible for him.

He knew he was falling for Sevda, but on the other hand accepting this was like betraying Mia and their unborn child. He was still holding himself responsible for their death and this was the prime reason he wanted to stay away from Sevda but staying away from Sevda wasn't easy for him. Since losing Mia, Sevda was the first woman he enjoyed being with. He was carrying her scarf on his elbow, as she had asked him to; he smelled it when he thought of her, but he still didn't know if he would get together with her again.

CHAPTER XXXXV

Kurt woke up as the airplane was landing at the Los Angeles airport. Before getting off the plane, he said to the flight attendants and pilots, "Thank you very much for thinking of me."

They all smiled, "We love to see you always on our flights, Professor."

After passport control, Kurt took a rideshare to Carol and Joe's house to pick up Junior. Junior was laying on the floor and looking sad. Kurt opened his arms and called to him. He stood up right away and ran to him. Kurt petted him a while and thanked Carol. He rode back home, and after taking a shower, he fed Junior, answered his email and text messages. He called Scott, "Hello Scott, I came back several hours ago. I just want you to know I'll be on time for tomorrow's schedule."

Scott said, "It's very nice to hear from you again, Kurt. We missed you very much. During your absence we rescheduled some operations for your return because we knew we couldn't handle them without you. You did a hell of a job saving that model on the Indonesia flight. It was a remarkable job. I read a copy of your report. This was very positive PR for our university. Everybody in the clinic is gossiping about your Turkish girlfriend. The photo of you holding hands is all over the internet. By the way, she looks beautiful. I am glad you are feeling better."

Kurt didn't know what to say. It was the last thing that he wanted to talk about with his coworkers. Kurt said, "It's a long story, we probably will talk about this later. Please give my love to your family. See you tomorrow." Kurt was very happy to cut the talk short. He took Junior on a walk at the shore, but even this long walk didn't help him to get rid of Sevda from his mind.

A week after he returned to Los Angeles, Kurt received an email from Sevda that said, "Dear Kurt, after you left Istanbul, it wasn't easy to go back to my daily life. I am still struggling in your absence. Monday, I went to the Anadolu Hisari municipal office, and they were very helpful in investigating your mom Ece's last name and shop. They found an Ece that owned a gift shop about forty-five years ago. Her name was Ece Ozgur. That building was demolished thirty years ago. A new office and store building have taken its place. They checked the records to see if there was anybody related to her with the last name of Ozgur who is living in Anadolu Hisari, but no one was identified in the records. There are at least more than a million people in Turkey with the same last name. If you want me to further research this, I can hire a professional person to help. I am sorry I couldn't help you much. I am looking forward to seeing you again soon. With love, Sevda."

CHAPTER XXXXVI

Kurt felt sad after reading Sevda's email. It wasn't easy to find his relatives in Turkey. This was the first time he felt that Sevda was sorrowful since he got to know her. Even though Kurt felt the same feelings as Sevda, he could never express to her how he felt. He didn't know how to do it anyway. He decided to respond to her email, "Dear Beautiful, since I came back to Los Angeles, I am working to catch up with the intense schedule they put me on. Thank you very much for researching my mom's past. I don't think further action is needed to investigate my mom's relatives. If I come back to Istanbul, I am sure I will one day try to look after my relatives again. The days we spent together were some of the best days I've had. Whenever I take a break between surgeries, I dream about the places we went. I guess it's become a form of dream therapy for me. If you take a trip to Los Angeles, you can stay at my place. I have a one-bedroom home with a big saloon and semi-studio. I am not at home most of the time because I am staying at the hospital. When I come home, I sleep in the saloon across from the TV, so you would have your own bedroom. Junior would love this too. He would like to have you at home and walk with you at the ocean side. Next weekend I'll have a three-day break. I planned a trip with Junior to the Imperial Wildlife preserve. We will listen to the animals, look at the stars and dream about those we love. Kurt."

Sevda couldn't believe what she read. Kurt was inviting her to Los Angles to stay with him. Most importantly, he was talking about his private life, and Kurt's happiness at being with her. She decided to fly to Los Angeles as soon as possible, but first she had to hire someone to take care of her business in her absence. She called her mom and told her about her plan to go to Los Angeles. Her mom had been expecting this although it came earlier than expected.

Sevda was so busy with her preparations for Los Angeles that she forgot to answer Kurt's email.

Kurt was on his way home after a busy week at work to prepare for his Imperial wildlife trip. His mind was going back and forth between Mia and Sevdas images. His feelings of responsibility for Mia's assassination by the terrorists were hurting him badly; on the other hand, Sevda's lively existence was bringing him back to life. With all these feelings, he found himself at home. There was a big oblong box in front of his door. He checked the box and saw that it was from Sevda. He took it in the house and opened it up. He couldn't believe his eyes. It was the vintage original Martin D-45 guitar she had given him. She had carefully attached a card in between the strings.

Kurt opened it up and read the card, "Kurt, when you open the package, this guitar will be in the hands of the person who deserves it. With all my heart, I want you to hold this. I am sure you will remember me when you play this. Love you, Sevda." She was a woman who expressed her feelings very easily, and Kurt was very happy with her attitude.

Kurt decided to respond to her gift with a gift when he came back from his weekend trip. He had a lot of time to think about what he could send her. He prepared his camping bags, then took Junior to drive to Imperial Wildlife. Kurt reserved a two-seat "Desert Quad" bike for this trip to El Centro. Early in the morning he stopped at the store to rent it. They had the bike on the trailer, and they hooked the trailer to Kurt's Ford Raptor, then Kurt and Junior drove to the Imperial Valley.

CHAPTER XXXXVII

Sevda woke up in the middle of the night to her phone buzzing. She was shaking not because the phone was buzzing, but because she was having a nightmare. The caller's ID showed her friend Deniz's name. She responded with fear, "Hi Deniz, what's going on?"

Deniz didn't sound well, "Did you watch the nightly news channel? There is news you might want to see." Sevda turned the TV on right away and saw herself on the channel walking out of the restaurant hand in hand with Kurt. The anchor was saying, "Everybody knows him as a cowboy and the surgeon who saved our lovely model Sevda by donating his blood on a flight. He had an accident yesterday, and he is in intensive care in an induced coma. He won our hearts when he visited Istanbul, and we are all praying for our hero Doctor West."

Sevda couldn't breathe and she wasn't able to talk with Deniz. She felt like she was going to be unconscious. She blamed herself, "I should have answered his email right away and told him about my plans to fly to Los Angeles next week." She realized that she should be strong and find a way to fly to Los Angeles in the morning. She knew sitting in her apartment and crying wouldn't help him or her. She decided to be with him and have him feel that she was there.

First, she called her mother and father. They had heard the news as well. She told them that she planned to fly to Los Angeles in the morning. She said, "I don't know when I'll be back. Can you please take care of my business and my apartment during my absence?" Her mother and father both said, "Of course."

Her father said, "You just get ready. I'll call my travel agent to find a ticket for you. I'll pick you up early in the morning to drop you off at the airport. If you need anything else, send me a text. We love you."

Her father was waiting for her early in the morning with a cup of coffee. She prepared only one carry-on and one checked luggage. She was dressed up in jeans and boots. Kurt loved to see her like that. Her father said, "Your flight ticket is ready at the airline counter. I reserved a hotel room right by the university hospital. Yesterday we found out that they transferred him to the Los Angeles University medical school surgery department. I think his colleagues are taking care of him." Her father dropped her off at the airport. Before she got inside, the press and paparazzi surrounded her. She politely asked for their support and told them she was flying to Los Angeles to see Kurt.

The airplane landed fourteen hours later in Los Angeles. She passed passport control and took a rideshare to the hotel. The hotel was walking distance to the hospital. She took a shower and put on light makeup, then walked to the hospital. Her heart was beating like crazy. She walked up to the surgery department intensive care unit check-in desk. She asked the nurses for Dr Kurt West's room. The nurses were adamant and didn't give any information or allow her to enter the intensive care unit.

She didn't know what to do, then a doctor approached her and said, "Hello. I heard you were asking for information on Kurt. My name is Dr Scott Smit. I guess I know you from your pictures with Kurt. You both became celebrities in Los Angeles as well. I am glad you came to see Kurt."

She smiled and said, "I am glad you saw me. I didn't know what to do. When I heard the news, I took the first flight to Los Angeles and came here."

Scott said, "Please come with me, I will take you to his room."

They walked to Kurt's room. Kurt was sleeping deeply and attached to a non-invasive ventilation device. He was sleeping calmly. Sevda collapsed into a chair and began to cry. Dr Smit said, "It's not as bad as it looks. Come with me. I'll buy you a coffee at the cafeteria and explain what happened."

Smit got two coffees and they sat down at a remote table. The other doctors and nurses appeared to recognize Sevda from the pictures. They looked at them and smiled. Scott said, "Sunday afternoon I got a phone call from the El Centro emergency hospital. They had Kurt wounded at their intensive care unit. I asked them immediately to transfer him with a medevac air ambulance here, and they did so. When we checked his vitals, he was stable, but sleepy. We found out that he had moderate brain trauma, and dehydration. We decided to put him into an induced coma. We are expecting that he has moderate brain swelling because of the head injuries, which can put pressure on his brain and could reduce blood flow and oxygen supply to the brain tissue. Inducing a coma sounds scary, but it decreases the brain's electrical activity, and metabolic rate. Ultimately, this helps decrease brain swelling and protects the brain from further damage. We will keep him in a coma for two more days. You are the only one right now who knows what happened to him. When they found him, his desert vehicle rolled over, and he was tied to the seat belt. Thank God he had a helmet on, and Junior was with him. Probably during the rollover, Junior jumped from the vehicle and waited a while before he sought help from other campers. We estimate that he stayed like that for two to three hours, but Kurt is a very tough man, and life hasn't been easy for him, but he survived again. Thanks to Junior. Junior is staying with Carol and Joe. We brought him a steak as a reward."

They were both silent for a while then Sevda said, "If you don't mind, can I stay with him?"

Scott said, "That would be very nice. He was talking very positively about you. I don't know how much you know about our Kenya–Somalia incident. Me and my family, and nurses Liz and Suzy—we are his family. Suzy and Liz stay with him during the nights. During the day, I check on him often. You are welcome to join us. In fact, I am one hundred percent sure he would be much happier to see you when he wakes up." Scott's cordial and warm demeanor calmed Sevda down. Scott said, "I will ask for a sleeper couch to be placed in Kurt's room, so you can rest when you get tired."

CHAPTER XXXXVIII

Sevda was sitting by Kurt and holding his hand when she recognized the scarf she gave Kurt in Istanbul. It was tied to his left elbow where she placed it. She had given it to him to bring him luck. In the evening, Nurse Liz came. She was a nice and pretty woman. She introduced herself to Sevda. After talking for some time about her memories with Kurt, Nurse Liz took Kurt's blanket off to replace it with a new one and massaged him. Sevda couldn't believe what she saw. Kurt's upper body, both front and back, were full of scars. The minute she saw it, she began to cry.

Liz gently touched her shoulder and said, "This happened after he saved our lives. He is a real hero, and nobody knows. He never takes off his shirt in public. He never tells anybody what happened during his captivity. Obviously, he was under intense torture by the terrorists. We never forget what he did for us. After he lost his wife Mia and unborn child, me, Suzy, and Professor Smit became his family. You look like a smart and openhearted woman. Obviously, you love him, and hopefully you will join our family."

Sevda hugged Nurse Liz and said, "I love him so much, and he is always on my mind every second, every minute, every hour, every day. If anything happens to him, I don't know how I can live without him. He is in me. I carry his blood. Like you said, he saved my life as well. Yes, I am his family."

Nurse Liz said, "I am glad you feel that you are his family like us." Then she smiled.

Sevda said, "I know I am not a nurse, but if you don't mind, I can clean his upper body. I know if I do that, he will start to feel that I am here with him."

Nurse Liz said, "Of course, those are the sterile towels."

Nurse Liz began to clean Kurt's lower body and massage him softly, then she quietly left the room. Sevda cleaned Kurt's upper body with sterile towels. After she finished, she started to touch every scar on Kurt's body. Tear drops were rolling down her cheeks. She softly talked into Kurt's ear and told him important details about her life that Kurt didn't know. She told him how much she loved him. She kept talking for several hours. When she became tired, she put her head by his hand and slept.

Early the next morning, Nurse Suzy came in with a cup of coffee and a croissant. She gently woke Sevda up and introduced herself. She said, "While you eat breakfast, I'll do the morning clean up. I heard many good things about you. After I finish cleaning, you can take a shower if you want. Today they'll wake Professor West up."

Sevda said, "Oh God, I am very excited to see him awake. Okay, I'll go to the hotel to take a shower and change. I'll be back in an hour."

Sevda returned to the hospital in a couple of hours. When she got to Kurt's room, she couldn't believe her eyes. They had already removed the respiratory devices and Kurt was breathing on his own, but he wasn't awake yet. There was only one intensive care nurse in the room, and she said, "Dr Smit removed the respiratory devices one hour ago, and he said Kurt was doing good. He should wake up soon."

Sevda said, "Oh my, this is very good news, thank you." She sat by Kurt and grabbed his hand and talked into his ear. Suddenly she felt Kurt's hand softly squeezing hers. Her heart started to beat fast. She didn't stop talking.

CHAPTER XXXXIX

Finally, with a smile, Kurt opened his eyes and looked at her flabbergasted. Sevda said with a big smile, "Hello cowboy."

Kurt responded to her, "Hello, Beautiful."

It was a pivotal moment for her. She softly kissed him on the lips, put her head on his chest and started to cry.

Kurt touched her hair with his hand and said, "I heard you when you talked into my ear. I loved every word you said. I am glad you are here, and I am very happy to see you when I wake up. I couldn't believe you were here when I first saw you. I thought it was a dream."

She couldn't believe what she heard. This was the first time she had heard such loving words from him. She said, "I love you, Kurt. I love you so much, and I regret not flying back to Los Angeles with you."

Kurt said, "Don't talk like that. I will tell you what happened to me after I leave the hospital. I have

to talk to Scott, and the others who took care me. They will probably discharge me as early as tomorrow. I hope you bought a one-way ticket to Los Angeles."

She hugged and kissed him again, and said, "You bet I did. I carry your blood in my veins." They both started to laugh.

Scott came in with a big smile on his face and explained how they treated him. "As far as I can see, tomorrow morning you can walk out of here. You should be able to come back to work in a week. By the way, you are very lucky to know Sevda. The entire department is impressed with her." Sevda blushed at his words.

Kurt responded, "I know how lucky I am. Such a tragic coincidence turned into happiness."

Sevda couldn't believe what she heard. Yes, this was the happiness she was waiting for. Yes, those were the kind of words she was waiting to hear from Kurt.

They gave Kurt a sedative to rest him overnight. Early in the morning, Sevda couldn't believe her eyes. Kurt was awake and ready to be discharged. He was waiting for Sevda with his discharge papers.

Scott came in, "Good morning, things are looking good with Kurt, so we are discharging him today. The paperwork will be ready in a couple of minutes. Kurt, please don't come back to work in two days. I will be waiting on you next week Monday. Your schedule will be busy, so I want you to be well rested, because I am taking a two-week break. I am sure this pretty woman will be happy to see you more." They all smiled.

The nurse came in with discharge papers and a wheelchair. Kurt smiled and sat on it. "Rules are rules and the same for everybody." The nurse pushed him to the hospital front door. Their rideshare car was waiting for them there. Kurt grabbed Sevda's hand for the first time before she could grab his. She looked at him with a big smile.

Kurt said, "Let's go home, get my truck and pick up Junior."

Sevda said, "That works for me. I am excited to see Junior as well."

CHAPTER XXXXX

Kurt showed his place to Sevda before they got in his truck. Sevda was impressed with Kurt's place. Nothing was excessive. He only had essential furniture.

Kurt said, "This is the bedroom where you can stay and sleep. I usually sleep on the couch in the saloon when I stay at home. Junior will be happy with you. He is probably bored alone at home."

Sevda turned to Kurt and said, "I have a hotel room by the hospital, and I was planning on staying there."

Kurt said, "No more separation, Sevda. I feel very happy with you, and I don't want you to stay at the hotel."

Sevda and Kurt kissed. They were hungry for each other's love, and they couldn't resist their bodies' desire. They made love for several hours without interruption. Sevda was kissing Kurt's scars and Kurt was kissing every part of Sevda's body. They both were racing to show each other how thirsty they were for each other's love.

As evening approached, Kurt softly kissed Sevda and said, "Let's go pick up first your luggage then Junior and grab a pizza on our way back home."

She burst into loud laughter, "I am ready."

They first picked up Sevda's luggage from the hotel and then drove to the doggie daycare. Carol opened the door for Kurt and

Sevda. Junior was looking at the door. The minute he saw Kurt, he jumped on him and started to lick his face.

Kurt said, "Look, Junior, this young and beautiful lady is Sevda. She is a dog lover like me. I am sure you'll love her." Junior approached Sevda and started to touch her with his nose. He smelled her then sat down by her. Kurt said, "He likes you, Sevda, like every other person. You will be good friends." On the way back home, they grabbed a pizza, and rewarded Junior with a big hamburger.

Sevda woke up in the middle of the night to the sound of a loud scream. Kurt wasn't in bed. She got out of the bed and walked to the activity room. Kurt was laying on the sofa, probably having a bad dream, most likely a nightmare. Junior was sitting by the couch quietly. She took a towel and started to clean Kurt's face and body. His body was strained, and all his muscles were contracting. She kissed him softly and woke him up. "Come with me to bed. Whatever you were seeing wasn't real. It was only a bad dream. I am here with you, and this is real love." She stretched her body toward him then kissed him. She gave him all her beauty and he joined her.

They only got of bed to eat something or walk Junior along the beach for the next four days.

Kurt said, "Love, I am thinking of driving together, first to Imperial Valley where the accident happened, then to Tucson to show you our ranch and

where I grew up."

She jumped into his arms and said, "I love this plan." She opened Kurt's closet and saw there were only five pairs of jeans, three pairs of boots, two jackets and seven shirts. She couldn't believe this. She had three closets full of clothing and shoes. She felt a little ashamed of herself. Kurt was a modest person. In contrast, she felt she was the spoiled one.

Kurt came into the room with a hat and a pair boot on and aid, "I ordered this Stetson hat, and Lucchese boots for you. Can you please try them?" The hat and boots fit her head perfectly.

She kissed Kurt and said, "Thanks."

They loaded into the Raptor, got Junior and hit the road.

Kurt said, "I want to teach you to drive this truck. You are a good driver. I witnessed it in Istanbul. We will take road trips sometimes, so we can share the drive."

CHAPTER XXXXXI

They were at the Imperial Valley by that afternoon. Kurt said, "Before we camp, let's drive to the area where the accident happened." They parked when they saw the accident tread marks. They walked along Kurt's driving route. Fifteen minutes later, they were horrified. There was an almost fifty-foot cliff in front of them.

Sevda wrapped her arms around him. "Oh Kurt, please don't put yourself in danger like this again. If anything happens to you, I can't live without you."

Kurt kissed her and said, "Let's go back and set up our tent at my usual campsite. I'll explain what happened to me here and in Somalia. I guess it's time, and you deserve to know, love."

Sevda said, "Thanks, Kurt, but you don't have to. I love who you are. I don't expect any explanation from your past. If you want, I'll be more than happy to listen to you, and I am grateful you consider me your partner."

Kurt folded his hands around her and kissed her.

They prepared their tents on the campground. While Kurt was feeding Junior, Sevda prepared dinner.

After dinner and a couple of beers, Kurt said, "Somalia's long captivity, and consistent torture left me with deep trauma. Abdul and

I woke up every night with nightmares. We were planning to escape them. It took years to find an opportunity. We ran away from them but after a couple of hours, they came within shooting range. One of their bullets hit me in the abdomen, which slowed us down dramatically. I asked Abdul to leave me and save himself, but he didn't. We saw a zebra herd, so we ran toward them. While we were running through the zebras, I asked for their help and a miracle happened. They opened like a crescent, and we ran in. They closed again and resumed grazing. We laid down and waited for some time. Abdul patched up my wound. I was losing blood and we didn't have anything to treat me. I asked Abdul to run by himself to find help for me, which he did. I don't remember anything after that until I saw the Kenyan officers and Abdul. They carried me to the chopper. I survived because of the zebras. Dreaming of Mia and our child gave me the strength to stay alive.

"The second strange encounter with animals happened while I was in Bali hiking with my Indonesian guide Ahmad in the Munduk jungle. We encountered a young Sumatran tiger. Ahmad aimed his gun at the tiger to shoot it, but I didn't allow him to. I looked into the tiger's eyes and talked to her. We were looking into each other's eyes, and I told her about our good intentions, so the tiger walked away. The third one happened after I came back to Los Angeles from Turkey. Junior and I were riding the desert bike were the accident happened. I began to drive a little bit faster and suddenly a longhorn herd cut my path. I swerved and the bike rolled over. I was lucky that Junior was with me. I don't remember but he found the other campers and saved me. As far as I understand, I stayed half-conscious for two hours. During these two hours, I dreamed of you. I dreamed of your smiling face, how you never gave up on me, your vulnerability, your elegance and most of all, your beauty inside and out. I was semi-conscious until they put me in an induced coma. I don't remember anything after that, but I do remember you talking into my ear and I felt your touch, and I could smell you. As you seen those animals prevented me fall of from deep cliff. I don't know if all these things were coincidences, or miracles, but I do know I love you, Beautiful."

She stood up from her chair and jumped toward him. "I love you, Kurt. Please don't leave me alone and do something dangerous again. I can't live without you. You totally changed my life, ever since the first time I saw you on the airplane. I was living in a dream before you, but you woke me up with your confident and lovely full voice when you said to me, 'Hello Beautiful.' That moment was my second birthday. I fell from a cliff, lost my boyfriend, lost my baby. I had no strength to fight back again but knowing a person like you totally changed me right away. You took such a big risk and gave me your blood even though you shouldn't have. You became my hero. The more I know you, the more I read about you, the more I fall in love with you. You are not only my hero, but you are everybody's hero. If you think you left me in Istanbul and go away to Los Angeles, the answer was no, because I would never allow you the leave me like that. I would only let you leave me, if you would look into my eyes and say I don't want you. I was preparing to move to Los Angeles to become close you. I don't know if these are coincidences or miracles. God, I love you so much."

Kurt stood up and grabbed her hand. "Come, let's get into the tent. I will teach you to make love like a cowboy."

She laughed, "I am already a cowgirl."

They made love all night long. Kurt didn't hear the desert animals howling. They were quiet all night long, including Junior. His hidden and confidential

friends were likely approving of Kurt's and Sevda's love. The next morning, Kurt woke up to the smell of coffee, and an omelet. He got out of the tent and saw that Junior was eating bacon.

Sevda said, "Good morning, cowboy. Looks like you are late today."

Kurt said, "Yes love, I slept comfortably for the first time in a long time, I guess it's the effect of love. Thanks for the beautiful breakfast."

They loaded the truck after breakfast, and Kurt said, "We are driving to Tucson today. If we get a chance, I will teach you how to country and barn dance. You will especially love my barn dance," then Kurt began to laugh.

Sevda began to country dance in her seat, "I love it, cowboy."

They hit the road to share their love forever.

AUTHOR BIOGRAPHY

Al Guner was born 1950 in Istanbul, Türkiye. After becoming a dentist in Türkiye, he moved to Germany for school. During that time, he was offered a postgraduate training program by the Department of Surgery Karl-Franzens University Graz, Austria. After completing the training program, he received a maxilla facial surgery fellowship offer. Unexpected health problems forced him to return to Türkiye. He completed his military duty in the Turkish army as a medical lieutenant. Thereafter Al became a partner in a music company in Istanbul, Türkiye. Eventually Al sold his shares in the company to EMI-London. In 1989 Al moved to Tucson, Arizona with his family. He now lives in Tucson with his wife.